The Fisherwoman and other stories

Thomas,

Enjoy the stories.

May the help your imagination

travel far,

Congrats.

Phil

The Fisherwoman and other stories

Philip Charter

Contents

The Fisherwoman

This is your fourth visit to the botanical biosphere. An invisible force pulls you in, even though you have only one hour of leisure time today. You scan your wristband and enter the soaring glass dome.

The biosphere teems with plants and trees. Mechanical bees flit between the groups of coloured flowers. Today, you've come to breathe in the life-giving humidity of the rainforest exhibit, but first, you pass through the Japanese gardens.

An elderly woman sits on a bench, overlooking the koi pond you like. The white-orange fish swim around in their docile dream, barely causing a ripple. She's been on that same seat each time you've come here. The chatter of other visitors filters through the bushes which shelter the pond from the main pathway.

You clear your throat. 'Hello, there.'

She looks up with kind eyes as if she'd been expecting someone. 'Yes, luvvie?'

'I noticed you often come to look at—'

'The fish? So beautiful,' she says. 'Blissfully ignorant of what's around them.' She coughs into a handkerchief and smiles apologetically.

The woman is right. Those fish exist within the confines of their pool, just as the vast majority of citizens live their entire lives in one place, their movements monitored and logged. You're one of the lucky ones who can travel.

'It's my medicine, see?' she says, gesturing with her hand. 'Three hours every day because of the grey-lung.'

One day, it'll be you on that bench with a prescription for natural air. When you ask if you can join her, she shifts to create more space and pats the seat next to her. You wonder if she remembers life before The Federation and if she was part of the nomadic workforce like you. She's mysteriously familiar. Is her *homestory* anything like yours?

When you were born, a unique piece of code was added to your identity chip. Everyone has one. The Scribe, The Federation's supercomputer, generates a narrative code based on individual DNA. The code holds your *homestory*. It must not be recorded, only recounted — shared when the human connection is strong enough to do so. As you sit, you decide to share yours with the woman in the Japanese gardens. She looks like an older version of you, same broad nose, same thick hair. She radiates an aura of calm.

'Can I share my story?'

She looks straight ahead at the koi pond. 'Of course.'

So many times you've folded a piece of paper and left it to be found, your unwritten story inside. But if discovered, it would be eradicated, so you never wrote it. You once found a *homestory* in an air duct you were upgrading. The dots and dashes of Morse code spattered the wall. Transcribing a few sentences each day thrilled you. Words coursed through your veins. It's probably been erased by now.

Others try to blurt theirs out to everyone they meet, but it's rare for you to tell your story. You face the woman and begin. 'My tale is that of The Fisherwoman, born hundreds of years ago, on an isolated island.'

The woman sits a little straighter. Perhaps she remembers a time when the sea surrounded land completely. When they connected the last island via earth bridges built by the bot fleet, The Federation announced it with much fanfare.

'While her husband went in search of new lands,' you say, 'she would fish the wide ocean inlets and the deeper trenches contained within the brilliant blue reef. Her people called the island The Jewel of Giants, as though her corner of the Earth was held together in the turquoise necklace of some greater being.'

The old woman sits with her hands on her knees, head tilted, interrogating each sentence for meaning. The irrigation system nearby puffs a light mist.

'In her boat,' you continue, 'she took a net, a flask of water, a hat for when the sun beat strong, and a pail for her catch.'

In your world, no personal possessions exist, not even flasks of water.

'Each day she fished in a different place, casting her circular net high. She watched it drift down into the sea. While she reeled it in, she hummed the tunes her mother had taught her, loud enough to become part of the soundscape, but not so loud she scared away the fish. With her pail full, she would return to the village.'

You've never tasted fish. Animal consumption is illegal. The last wild animals perished and huge droves of insects now roam the Earth. Modern cereals are immune to them, other plants are not. Unfarmable areas grow oxygen-producing bushes, designed to poison all pests. The Federation exists in perpetual chemical warfare with its own land.

'And when do the giants come?' the woman asks.

You're surprised she interrupted. 'Have you heard it before?'

'I know it from another perspective.'

Your heart swells. If her narrative connects, she might be a blood relative — a great aunt, or a second cousin. You've never met a relative before, although you've spent many nights wondering where they are.

'Sorry,' she says. 'I'm holding you up.'

There may not be time to visit the Amazonian biodome, but it's more important you deliver the *homestory* as best you can. You gather yourself and continue.

'After many months away, her man returned and together they raised a baby girl. She took the child fishing in her canoe, hoping that the songs she hummed would pass down, along with the joy of being a fisherwoman. They lived happily until one day men in bigger boats arrived at their island.'

As a child, you lived underground in an orphanage. Days passed in geometric routine, with no time allocated to discover or dream. They said you were fortunate to learn a trade and provide a service to the nomadic workforce of The Federation.

Your job in air filtration takes you all over the planet. Over the years, you've seen places you could never have imagined, heard the *homestories* of countless others — The Warrior Queen, The Great Bullion Thief, and The Deaf Maestro. But, with so much exposure to unfiltered air, your lungs won't last.

'These men were giants, their hands callused from strong wooden oars,' you say.

As if to participate in the story, one of the fish comes up for air and splashes water from the pool.

'They towered above the fisherwoman, covered with dark tattoos. Wooden bars skewered their ears. The men destroyed her village. Roofs burned to black in seconds and the smell of smoke tarnished the air forever. They killed her husband and took her baby. Before they thrust a spear into her belly, the fisherwoman held up her hand and cried 'Wait!'. The men paused. 'I will show you where the fish run,' she said. 'This island has a bountiful supply, but only I know where.'

You try to imagine tropical fish. Were they flat and smooth, like the rays in the great botanical gardens of Singapore, or silvery and fast, like the shoals of mackerel in the Nordic Aquarium? You've visited so many public ecosystems, but the Japanese gardens are your favourite. Their gentle flow draws you in and holds you here, like you are part of its DNA. You feel one step closer to the fisherwoman.

The old woman hangs her head, as if sensing further tragedy, but however her story links with yours, it can't interrupt the end of your tale.

'She showed the men her fishing spots and they brought endless nets from their ships. The nets tore the coral from the sea bed and dragged up creatures big and small. While they worked, she hummed the songs she loved, but in her head. The men rejoiced at the size of the larger fish and laughed at the smaller ones. They ate them all until there were none.'

The wristband on your arm vibrates. Five minutes until the ticket expires. You quicken the pace of the story.

'After a time, the fishing grounds ran dry and the men left in search of new territory. The seas lay still, and nothing grew in the scorched ground. The remaining villagers survived on coconuts and dry roots. This was the fisherwoman's punishment for saving herself.'

When you look up, the woman is crying. Crystal teardrops splash the ground below.

'Don't cry,' you say. 'It's only a fable.'

She wipes the tears away with a sleeve. By now, her aura of calm breaks. Her voice shakes. 'I know, luvvie. I know how it ends.'

It doesn't matter that your ticket is running out and you won't visit the rainforest exhibit. All you want is for the woman next to you to witness the end of the story, and to discover why it affects her. Were you destined to meet? Orphans can go a whole lifetime without finding the stories which connect to theirs.

In solidarity, you close your eyes and live the fisherwoman's past and future. Her song grows louder and clearer each time. You breathe her air and bear the burden of her decision.

'Wait,' the woman says. 'Before you finish, I have to show you this.' She stands, lifts her right foot onto the seat and rolls up her trouser leg. Etched onto her calf is a small tattoo; its piercing colours contrast with the metal bench. The image shows a woman in a broad hat, paddling her boat through blue waters. Barely visible at the back of the canoe is a young girl holding a pail.

Your wristband vibrates again but you ignore the warning.

Now you understand what draws you back to the Japanese gardens. A lump swells in your throat. You want to live this moment forever, and cry together with the woman from your *homestory*.

Before you can speak, she continues your story.

'In trying to save herself, the fisherwoman had ensured the death of something more important. For that, she was stricken with guilt.'

She dabs at her face with a sleeve.

'One day, she paddled her canoe far into the ocean until she could not see land. She did not bring a hat, or a pail, or a flask of water.' She phrases the words exactly as you would.

The woman starts to hum a song but erupts into a coughing fit. Although she must be younger, she has the withered frame of an eighty-year-old.

You remove a tissue and guide her back into the seat. 'Relax now. Just rest.'

She agrees and you finish the story.

'Visitors to that place maintain that if you hold your ear to the wind on the shores of her island, you can hear the faint humming of the fisherwoman's song.'

Each and every time you recount The Fisherwoman, you leave a part of yourself behind with it. It exhausts you, but builds a desire to hear the story of the person you shared it with. Especially this time. Moving closer, you reach for your biological mother's hand. There is no more time to hear which forces took her away and how her *homestory* connects to yours. Not today.

You help her to her feet and embrace the woman you've waited your whole life to meet. You are both part of this place, at one with the koi and the cherry trees of the Japanese gardens. She must stay and you must leave.

'I'll come back soon,' you say. 'You can tell me your story next time.

Two Minutes, Forty-Six Seconds

Guitars raged, notes bathed in distortion. Fifty bodies packed tight to the stage soaked up the rumble of bass. Cymbals smashed like breaking ice; the aircon unit didn't have a chance against the heat. Feet shuffled between songs, and the singer screamed or talked or didn't say anything. Tending bar, I listened to every furious track run out of gas just before the three-minute mark. My bar.

Later, when the band finished and the drinkers left, I went to the back office and played records on the turntable until sunrise. At that time of day, jazz calmed me. You didn't have to try and make sense of it. Pick up Pop's old guitar, play a few tracks before sleep — equilibrium. Everything then nothing. Cacophony then silence. That was how it went every night at Ortega's Bar, apart from Sundays visiting Mom in Queens.

I woke to the familiar hum of traffic on the Williamsburg Bridge. Ortega's gave me the sense of place I craved since Pop died and I moved out at sixteen. Close to thirty years I'd bounced around and dreamed of running a venue, but now, the only way to pay the bands a real wage was to sleep at work to avoid skyrocketing rents.

The place sat a few blocks from the river, and the sound of the bridge carried all the way to the back office. When I got my eyes open and hauled myself upright on the settee, I watched Beth toss an out-of-place beige coat on the bar. She inspected it for a tag then pulled on a pair of cleaning gloves.

'Thought I told you to come in later.' My head throbbed.

'It's already ten-thirty, boss.' She smiled and turned on the speaker system.

'No, don't you—'

Beth cranked up the volume and *It's Too Late* by The Dolls blasted out of the stereo. Her idea of a joke.

Big riffs blared and I covered my ears until she took pity on me and turned it down. I pulled on the Ramones shirt next to me and returned Pop's Gibson 335 to its case. 'Who owns the jacket?' I shouted. 'Sure ain't yours?'

'Do I look like a cosmopolitan-drinking Midtown lawyer?' she called back. Beth went back to scrubbing away the traces of the night before.

'Going for coffee,' I said on my way out.

It's a wonder I wasn't more out of shape — forty-eight years old with tar-filled lungs and 'getting some air' was my only exercise. The sky was heavy, but I still did the loop up to the East River and back. Stretch your legs down Fifth, turn onto Roebling and wait in line at the coffee shop. It occurred to me that New York scenes appear as album covers — street signs, shopfronts, groups of people, all frozen for a second in black and white.

Brooklyn now belonged to the twentysomethings with beanie hats and big headphones. Blindfolds for the ears is what the old man called them. The rhythm of these new conversations was the one type of street music that didn't make sense to me. Two tracks played at once as streams of discordant thoughts fought for space. So many words with so little said.

That evening, I met the owner of the long beige coat. She walked in with a briefcase and a tote bag, like she couldn't keep her work and personal life in just one. I gave her the trenchcoat and she inspected it for damage. It didn't suit her red hair, but it probably cost more than all the top shelf bottles combined. This woman was not a regular at Ortega's. In fact, I'd never seen her before. My regulars were younger hardcore music freaks who liked to write on the walls but didn't mind paying six bucks a beer. Her tote bag bulged with the outline of a seven-inch single. I imagined the vintage turntable in her meticulous apartment with its white walls and Scandinavian furniture. Maybe she had to listen to records before she could get to sleep, too.

When she tried the coat on, I half expected her to pull out a dictaphone and fire questions about licensing laws. Instead, she ordered a drink. 'Tequila, lime and soda, please.' She shook her head when I reached for the bottle of *añejo*. 'Just the regular stuff.'

'Alrighty,' I said, switching bottles. A moment of quiet. 'Enjoy the show last night, ma'am?' I pointed to the flyer for the gig: *The Dirty Jockeys.*

'Ain't no ma'am,' she said, ticking me off with a pointed finger. 'I'm Kristy, and I'm a new-wave punk, actually. Don't let the work clothes fool ya.'

Her accent screamed Brooklyn, abrasive but assured. She looked corporate but her attitude brought some light into my dark little bar. Most of the other girls in Ortega's wore nihilistic expressions and a lot of black.

As I faced the mirror behind the bar and fixed the drink, an older version of me stared back — stone-washed jeans, a half-grown beard, and my old man's silver chain resting over my t-shirt. Time to fraternize was a rarity. Every day before opening, I trawled the listings, booked bands, and checked the trendsetting blogs. Afternoons the office door stayed shut; my head buried itself in paperwork. The evenings ran on, pouring the drinks and agreeing with whatever opinions people offered. All on repeat.

'Anyway, I'm Daniel. Welcome to my underground kingdom.'

It wasn't a welcoming place, with its empty stage, wooden stools stickers peeling off the black walls, but the music mattered.

She looked around. 'You're *Daniel* Ortega? Like the president of that country?'

'Err, yeah. Nicaragua. I'm just the president of this place.'

She sipped her drink. 'Can't believe I never came here before last night. It's… nice.'

What did she mean by nice? It was a dive bar, an escape. That's the whole point.

'Well, I never hit the big time with my own music, so this place gives the other guys a chance.' My laugh sounded weak. The craving for a cigarette punched me in the chest.

She scanned the posters above the stage, perhaps imagining all the concerts over the years.

'Now then. Pick a song.' I pointed to the laptop behind the bar with the playlist. 'What ya' got?'

She thought awhile. 'What about something by Lost Acapulco?'

A smile. An easy one. *Mexican surf?* 'You sure got me profiled.'

My father once told me the story of how he arrived from Mexico and auditioned for Dick Dale's band, but he took a job in Queens instead, trading semi-stardom for a place in the *barrio*. I found the track and queued it up. 'Not sure this one could be described as a classic, but here we go.'

'Does it have to be a classic? Ain't it enough to just like something anymore?'

That made me laugh.

We listened to the twanging guitars and the shallow snare. All the stupid bands I'd played in flooded back. While Kristy drank, I told stories about the shittier venues. If only there was an Ortega's back then.

That night's band arrived and the place began to fill up. Soon, the clatter of glasses and distorted guitars interrupted our conversation, and Kristy picked up her jacket and walked out the door, back to whatever she'd been running from the night before.

That night, before sleep, I didn't listen to jazz records, ŏr play the guitar. I played that surf track and thought about how my pop taught me how to play tremolo style. Hours and hours repeating Dick Dale riffs. It almost drove my mother out onto the street.

***

The next couple of months I got tired of booking bands with 'new sounds' that weren't any different, and tired of new customers who always said the same things. Ortega's felt less like my place even though I slept there.

New York slipped away, too. The city played unfamiliar notes, and the soothing traffic on the bridge turned to angry static with no volume control. The far off clang of construction work on the factories turning themselves into hip apartments — noise, not music. Now, headphones accompanied me on my walks to block out the city's voices.

Beth and the rest of the staff took whisky shots and guitar riffs like pills, but the bar struggled against the cycle of finding 'the next big thing' in rock music. Bands I championed went on to sell out bigger shows, but Ortega's wouldn't let go of me. Kristy hadn't returned since that day. I even considered booking Lost Acapulco to get her back.

On the day of our annual staff party, I closed the bar and set out to get some air. The corner of Broadway and Bedford, opposite the fifty-foot mural of a disinterested girl, I passed a new street guitarist.

The focus on the guy's face made me stop and look. Headphones off, street sound on. That raw energy transported me back to the old New York of my teenage years.

The kid was African-American, about eighteen, sat on a beat-up Marshall amp hammering a black Les Paul. His Converse boots operated on a kick-drum cymbal combo. He had no sign, no CDs, the bumps and scratches on his guitar did all the talking. He tore through a medley of 70s classics — Dictators, Heartbreakers, The Void — and added his own licks in too. A dozen people gathered around but the young guitarist played hunched over, eyes fixed on the guitar neck. I lit a cigarette and let the sound wash over.

The street switched to sharp anti-color. The cars aged, pristine shopfronts turned to broken ones, and brick walls became a canvas for graffiti tags. My mind traveled back to those Queens nights. Six hours straight rehearsal in Rocco's lockup. My fingers screamed, but that didn't stop me flipping off passing cop cars on the way back.

He finished his set and I dropped a ten and a card for Ortega's into his case. 'Thanks for making me feel like I belong here again, kid. Give me a call if you ever want an opening slot.'

He cleared the street dust from his eyes. 'Awesome. Thanks, man.'

That music gave me the jolt I needed to revisit some old haunts. My walk took me the two miles across the East River into Lower Manhattan. I knew of The Mudd Club from the bootleg recordings in

Mom's attic but I'd never been because it closed in '83. Eventually, I found the memorial sign on the wall. All the ugly imperfections of that area had been remastered. Further down on Leonard Street, chauffeur-driven cars replaced the empty bottles and merch sellers that used to clutter the street. Venues like those were a connection to my father, but the sounds of that world were fading.

That evening, the party moved to a newer place: The Knitting Factory. At least the tunes would be classics. Beth and others deserved a thank you for their hard work at Ortega's, and a night out got me away from that place.

We did the usual, shooting tequila and pulling faces to the camera. The night went long. A covers band played an Undertones song and got me out of the booth. As I made my way to the dancefloor, a hand touched mine.

'Hey there, Mr. President.'

She looked thinner, with a little more makeup than before. No beige trench coat.

'Kristy.' I leaned in and kissed her cheek. 'You been blowing off my bar for this place?'

'No, this is my first night out for… well, not many of my friends are into this.'

Even if they didn't understand her music, she needed to hear it anyway. I admired that.

The band built up to the chorus of Teenage Kicks. 'We're the only ones old enough to know this one,' I shouted over the music. I lit an imaginary cigarette. 'Smoke?'

She nodded and exhaled as if she'd already taken a drag.

We went outside and talked. Well, she talked and I listened. She'd lost her mother. That explained the absence. I lit another cigarette and offered the lighter. Instead of taking it, she pinched the thing out of my mouth and took a drag. 'Don't smoke now,' she said with a smirk, 'but it doesn't count if it's yours.'

We listened to the muffled music and watched our cigarette smoke rise up like steam from the manhole covers.

'It's not like many people our age still do this.' She pointed at her oversized black t-shirt and handbag combo. 'Fortysomethings at rock bars…'

My shoulders shrugged. 'Guess it's another habit I can't kick.'

As we shared a smoke, she reached down and took my hand in hers. Middle-schoolers again. We stood there and listened to drowned out music and the traffic on wet Brooklyn streets. The time that passed was just sound over distance.

'Been feeling out of place of late,' I finally said. 'The changes around here never bothered me before, but recently—'

'I know, right? Don't recognize places.' A laugh escaped, but with the hint of a sob behind it. She gazed at the night sky, then took a final drag on my cigarette and killed it. '… You know I came back to the bar. Couple of Sundays, actually.'

My day off. 'I'm at my mom's on Sundays.' I remembered *her* mom too late.

'Oh, I guessed you had kids.'

Kids? As if I had a cozy house in the 'burbs and came into town to run my rock bar. 'I can't even keep an apartment, let alone a family.'

An easy laugh, natural with a long fade out.

The door opened, leaking unknown songs onto the street. A group came out to smoke vape pens.

'Got an idea,' she said. Her face brightened like a kid who had broken into the principal's office. My mind raced through the possibilities of where the evening might take us. 'Let's go somewhere old,' she said. 'Somewhere we can hear ourselves.'

Without me telling it to, my hand reached out and touched her arm. 'Sure thing.' It didn't matter if we ended up in an empty bar or an all-night diner, I wanted to make up for all the time I'd wasted chasing new sounds. 'As long as they've got tequila, I'm in.'

I zipped my jacket and we went off into the night.

***

It was spring and I was at Mom's for breakfast. Nothing much happened early on a Sunday, and we liked the quiet.

'Daniel… Danielito! Your *chilaquiles* are getting cold.' She shuffled over to scrape her own half-finished plate into the trash. Mom used to eat and the kitchen used to be less of a health hazard.

I looked up. 'Right. Thank you, Ma.' My fork clicked against the plate.

'What's up with you?' she asked. 'You're so distracted.'

A lack of balance was all.. 'Just enjoying the silence.'

She tucked her gray hair behind her ear so she could hear better. 'Your Papi used to say when the city's quiet, it's not an absence. Silence is a note, too.'

Her idea took a while to sink in. Take another mouthful. Chew. 'I like that.'

La Nueva 93.1 droned on in the background. The sun-bleached curtains in the kitchen were the same pair from my youth. My folks didn't have much when they moved here from Mexico, and my father was gone before they'd had the opportunity to move with the times. I guess my mom didn't like change either.

'You're so much like him.'

I looked up. 'Because of the music?'

'No,' she said, 'because you can't stay still. Always chasing what comes next.' Mom's eyes glazed over. 'He sure could play,' she said. 'Yes, he had a wonderful ear, but sometimes he couldn't hear what was right in front of him.'

Like Kristy and me. We didn't know what we were running from, till we told each other. I drained my cup of coffee and kissed Mom on the cheek. 'It's always nice to see you.' It seemed selfish to cut my visit short, but my days off were for Kristy now, too.

'Wait. There's something I want you to have,' she said.

While she went to collect it, I stacked the dishes. I heard her go through the piles of his junk she still kept in the living room. What a mess it would be once she couldn't live on her own anymore — nurses, medication and assisted-living bills.

She came back into the room empty handed.

'I thought you were—'

'Shhh,' she said.

Then, the first bars of a track I hadn't heard in a very long time came from the other room. I turned off the faucet to tune in better and buried the lump in my throat. My old man's limited-edition record played, the jazz one she didn't like to wear out. Why now? His archtop guitar flowed in and out of the mix while the singer's vocals drifted over the top. Mom turned up the volume on her stereo. We listened together in the kitchen to the crackles and pops as the needle dug into the grooves of the only copy left, slowly erasing the record each time it played. I put my arm around her and we looked out the window, remembering summer nights spent outside, dancing and hollering. That was before I turned into a teenager who said 'screw you' to everyone.

My father played his jaunty solo, tapping away at the notes. He brought style back into that tired old room. Those memories never came in black and white. In two minutes and forty-six seconds, New York Swing ended and the sound died. For a few seconds after, we listened to the note of silence.

'I want you to have it,' she said. 'Put the record above the stage so he can hear some new music.'

Now *that* was an idea. Build a display case for his guitar and print a photo. '*Gracias, Mamá.*'

That was all that needed to be said. I didn't need to tell her about Kristy, or my plan to step back from the bar. I didn't need to say that nowhere in this city felt like mine anymore, but that when the right track played and you were with the right person, it still sounded like home.

Mom sat quiet at the kitchen table and I went to get the record. The stylus lifted and the vinyl span on the turntable. Forty-five revolutions per minute. Around and around. I pressed stop.

Racing Fate

Charles Carrington
Happy Valley Racecourse, Hong Kong
February 26, 1918

Squinting through the multitude, I caught a glimpse of the favourite: a muscular grey. My man on the mainland thought him a certainty for the China Stakes. As the murmurings of the spectators grew, my heart quickened, just as it had done before we charged into battle in Flanders. Thankfully, I had managed to outrun that particular conflict.

While I knew little about racing, I'd never been afraid of risking my hand. You can do that when you've experienced what it's like to have nothing; when you've seen the man next to you cut in two by machine-gun fire and wondered why it was him and not you. I neglected to fight for a seat in the stands, so made do with a partially obscured trackside view. From there, I would watch as the horse took everything I had or solved most of my financial issues.

The cool greens of East Anglia were worlds away. The humid air in Happy Valley made one sluggish. Tall hills penned the circuit, with the 'grandstand' nothing more than a ramshackle bamboo structure. I fanned myself with the racecard, watching the couples deep in conversation and the groups of Chinese exchanging information and promises for banknotes. A newspaper photographer with his head under the cover trained his camera on the race day scene.

As I readied my final hundred-dollar notes to make the bet, I cursed my lack of support. My uncle, who had acted as my mentor and guide in the Orient, had used his half of the shipping company as collateral to secure credit, and then absconded. Just thinking about him holed up in some den of iniquity with my family's money made me shake with rage.

I took one final look at the runners and ventured towards a Chinese bookmaker and his apprentice.

'Carrington. Carrington, old boy.'

I turned to see Nathaniel Stone, heir to his father's sizeable trading company, waving a newspaper in my direction. His gut protruded over his trousers, however much he attempted to cover it by puffing out his breast.

'Nathaniel,' I said, tipping my hat as graciously as I could manage.

He slapped me on the shoulder. 'Missed you at the club last week. Got tired of losing at bridge?'

I longed to play cards with people other than clean-collared buffoons, but in Hong Kong, socialising with the right types was just as important as balancing your books. 'Had a few issues.'

He grinned. 'I heard about your uncle. The scoundrel!'

Despite the crowds, a silence lay between us.

'If you need anything, all you have to do is ask,' he said. Stone thrived on moments like that — offering crumbs to the starving to double his share of the crop in years to come. I wished I could have asked someone else, but my uncle had worn out all of our friends' good graces. Henrietta and the children might never be able to make the trip to join me unless my fortunes changed.

'Glad I can count on you, Stone. Us 'white devils' ought to stick together.'

Another silence.

My father's old pocket watch showed fifteen minutes to the off; ample time to make the bet. 'Could I borrow a sum for the big race? Got an iron-clad tip from a client of mine who trains horses up in The New Territories.'

In truth, the tip wasn't the only reason I had resorted to gambling. I'd seen a soothsayer in the market. A man in my predicament might have tried anything. He read my troubles through the unsteadiness of my hands and through my soldier's stare. He mentioned the significance of silver and told me that a high-odds game of chance would offer me salvation. And here I was, about to bet on the grey.

Stone removed his straw hat and fanned himself. 'How much are we talking?'

Papa and I would spend no more than a few shillings on the Grand National, but now I needed fast cash, shillings wouldn't do. 'Eight hundred dollars or so…'

His piggy eyes made their calculations. 'Quite the pickle you're in, Carrington.' Stone didn't know the half of it: interest payments, veiled threats from the Triads, and a court-martial awaiting me in England.

'Let's make it an even thousand dollars at three per cent monthly,' he said with another whack on the arm. One hundred pounds was no small sum of money. Stone, however, seemed unfazed. 'I'll wave the interest if you pay within a week.' He asked for the watch as a sign of good faith, not because it was worth anything, but because he knew I wouldn't leave it behind.

I wrote him a promissory note before he changed his mind. 'You know I'd do the same if—'

'Don't mention it, old boy. Just ensure you win the bloody wager.' He turned and left without asking the name of the horse I intended to bet my life on.

Jeffrey Huang
February 21, 2018

I checked again. The leather bag bulged, the money inside. It was all there, thousands in notes. The packed stands crackled and the lights burned bright on the concourse. My dream of owning a racehorse seemed both a certainty and an impossibility. After the next race, I'd finally know what it felt like to be more than a spectator in life.

That morning, Vanessa and I had gone over wedding costs for what felt like the tenth time.

'If we don't pay the next instalment we lose our deposit,' she said.

I earned a good salary as a senior shipping clerk, but she'd recently been made redundant. 'You know I've got some other savings,' I said.

'Jeffrey, I could never… you've had that since you were a boy.'

'We'll make it work, my love. You'll see.' I kissed her forehead and left for the office.

The money in my account was a legacy from Jack, my father, the man who had first taken me to the stadium on Hong Kong island. From the first time the hooves thundered past and the finishing-line fever built to red-hot, I was hooked. Investing the fund into the future of a living, breathing being would keep that connection alive.

With only a quarter of an hour to go, my blood pumped faster than the first time I ever watched a live race. Spectators in the grandstand sat with their heads buried in the form section of the South China Morning Post. I preferred to view the horses in the paddock, looking for signs that others missed. My holdall groaned, heavy with notes. The runners trotted out.

The events that led me to take my entire savings fund to the track started on the way to work. The first tram to arrive was the Eight, my lucky number. At the office, I received a phone call from a school friend who worked in the Lui stables up near Sha Tin. He was confident about the chances of their charge Born In China.

27

When I checked the racing section in the paper I found the perfect investment: a syndicate looking for a new member to buy into a promising three-year-old gelding of top-quality lineage. The name: Captain Jack. The share was half a million Hong Kong Dollars — way out of my budget, but I knew it was the one I'd been waiting for.

The horses entered the paddock one by one. Most were nervous and flighty due to the noise, sweating under the lights, but the favourite, Born in China, with his jockey in red and yellow silks, trotted nonchalantly, as if it were just another day. They had done a marvellous job preparing him for the trophy race; every muscle bulging, his coat gleaming silver.

The odds on the big screen across the turf were up. One point nine. I'd need to pair it with another runner in a two-horse quinella to make enough for the wedding costs and the syndicate buy-in. I unzipped the bag and stared at the bundles of notes inside. I'd be going home with it full or empty.

Charles Carrington

Before I could place the bet and take my place in the stand, I heard an almighty crash. It was a sound of war — the kind that would make even the most hardened veteran turn and run. The thunderous crack of the grandstand structure failing was joined by a siren of cries of the hundreds underneath. Upon turning, I saw the final stage of its collapse from three levels to one.

Shock. Paralysis. Confusion. We scrambled backwards to the rail, unable to take our eyes off the tragedy, unable even to draw breath. Debris flew and thick dust choked the air. When the last pole toppled, the orchestra of cries swelled to a horrifying crescendo.

A brave few ran towards the fractured mess of splintered bamboo and bodies, attempting to help those at the edge. A young vendor wearing a coolie hat emerged with a stout, bearded gentleman. The injured man screamed in agony as he tried to stand on a broken leg, and pointed back towards the pile. *'Ma femme! Mes enfants! A l'aide!'* The on-duty police formed a hasty cordon around the area to prevent further injuries.

Spectators formed a raging sea, rushing for the exit. I saw Stone clutching the rail, stripped of his usual self-confidence. During my conscription, I'd seen enough fresh Tommies to recognise a man witnessing his first death. I grabbed his collar and shouted above the panic. 'We've got to get in there and help. There'll be hundreds trapped.'

His gaze locked onto the horror of the flattened stands. 'It's too dangerous, man. We'll be crushed.' When I pulled at his wrist, he gripped the rail tighter.

I swore never to run from a battle, but I thought I'd never face such destruction and carnage again. Fighting against the current of the crowd, I reached the edge and peered in, looking for outstretched arms, straining my ears to hear the slightest call. Limbs and bodies scrambled from atop the mess, competing to reach the safety of ground level.

Smoke began to filter through from the back of the fallen stand where the food vendors had their carts. The sounds of those trapped became muffled and choked. Soon, the angry smell of burning raced over to those of us in the rescue effort. The Chinese vendor who had dragged the French man away removed his hat in a futile show of respect.

Rapidly advancing flames forced us to retreat several paces, then a few more. The blaze was fierce and before long, it ate up the bamboo, the wood, the food carts, and all of those poor souls trapped inside. Smoke rose high into the valley, above the mountains and out into the bay. I withdrew to the safety of the middle of the track, away from the awful sounds. Away from the smell. There was nothing I could do but watch through the waves of heat. It could have been me. It could have been my family. In around twenty minutes, the blaze had claimed everything and died its death. I was only minutes away from ruin that day, but for many, there would be no salvation.

Jeffrey Huang

The horses circled the paddock. Number One, Archippus, looked calm and capable. Purton was a champion jockey, but the horse was carrying too much weight. As I looked on, a hunched pensioner tapped me with his racecard. The front page read *Remembering Happy Valley: The centenary of a tragedy.* The man could have been a hundred years old himself, but his eyes still had that same race-night sparkle my father's had.

'Look at the grey horse,' he said. 'Nobody will beat those legs today.'

I smiled and tapped him back on the arm. 'You're right, old man. He's pure class and his stable says he's in peak condition. Not much money in the win stakes though.'

He observed me quizzically for even suggesting betting 'win'. It was the hundred-to-one combinations that kept racegoers like him coming back every week.

'Any other tips?' he asked.

'Follow your own signs,' I said. 'That's what my father used to say.'

As he went off to make his bet, I fixed my gaze on the Australian gelding coming next. House of Fun was anything but consistent, but the trainer, John Size, had been successful since moving to Hong Kong. The animal's slender legs twitched with every step and the steward riding alongside pulled hard at the reins to keep him straight. All of those punters watching a screen or with their head buried in the statistics missed the reality of racing — the pure animalism of the horses, the natural desire. Those sparks of nervous energy made the difference in sprint races and gave the mounts their staying power. The horse would run in stall number eight — another sign.

Inside, I filled out my betting form and stared down at the number of zeros. To Vanessa, racing was mathematical wizardry, but to me, it contained a beautiful order. Was I really going to do this? The clocks ticked down to race time and the queue inched forward.

Eventually, it was my turn at the window. The clerk snatched the paper and fed it into the machine. Just another bet. A message appeared on the clerk's screen and she turned and spoke to her manager. The manager glanced at the sheet in her hands — banned gamblers and suspicious odds. Even though the building was air-conditioned, the room was suddenly sweltering. Beads of sweat cascaded down my face.

The pensioner from the paddock appeared at the window next to mine. 'Now this must be a sign,' he said, looking at me as if I were a treasured family member. 'What are you going for?'

'Two and eight,' I replied, over the voices of the other gamblers. 'Betting my future on it actually.' Meanwhile, the clerk tapped on the glass to indicate her manager had approved the bet.

He looked back with a knowing smile. 'I've done that a few times.' He smoothed his chin with a steady hand. 'I'll go with two and eight as well.' The paper went to the clerk.

People behind me in the queue were getting impatient, inching forward to apply the pressure. I dropped the stacks of notes on the counter and slid them under the window.

The old man registered no surprise at the size of the bet. According to him, I was the wise one. He pushed his own pile of notes under the window and made his bet. The man stepped aside from the queue and nodded goodbye, leaving me alone with my ticket, the most expensive piece of paper I'd ever held.

Charles Carrington

For a good while, nobody spoke more than a few words. Police and ambulance men gave orders and we obeyed. Hours passed. The first encounter with charred remains or a faceless body showed on the expression of every volunteer. Darkness began to hamper our efforts clearing the debris, so we waited for the electric spotlights to arrive. That time shuffling around, waiting to find a survivor, someone who could be helped, took me back to those dark hours watching the German line. Not a soul would move but your mind played tricks every damned minute.

We formed a chain to separate the fallen structure from the people that had occupied it. Every now and then, a gust of wind kicked up the ash and sent everyone into coughing fits. Before long, my shirt blackened and a feeling of lightheadedness prevailed. All I'd had to drink was a few pulls on the brandy in my hip flask.

Ambulance men erected triage tents on the infield and loaded the wounded onto stretchers. Others were dumped into wooden carts to be identified later. The charred-flesh smell that came with them was something that would stay with me for ever. The death toll must have reached hundreds, and the wounded more like a thousand.

At some point, I rested on the grass. I had nothing more to give, so observed the blackened sky. When I'd arrived in Asia, the stars had offered the promise of a great future. Uncle's shipping business had been motoring along, and I'd soon found my feet with the expatriate British. I'd imagined the children going to school in hats to shield them from the sun. Henrietta would have enjoyed trips to the islands and walking along the shoreline. But now…

Hours later, I awoke to a chill, still on the grass in my smoke-stained shirt and trousers. Most had abandoned the rescue effort by the small hours. Staying would have been a meaningless gesture. Besides, the fire was a clear message about my future on the continent. While I hated playing the role of deserter once more, my only hope of seeing my family again depended on it. I dusted myself off and hailed a carriage to take me to the waterfront.

The thousand dollars Stone had lent me would buy a head start anywhere I chose. Hong Kong was filling up rapidly, and there was nothing left for me to put a flag in and call my own. Years from now, these hills would be covered in buildings. I was destined to leave before then.

The tragedy would provide ample cover for me to slip away from my creditors. Stone was the only soul who knew I hadn't been taken by the fire, and I would see to it that his money was repaid when I got on my feet. I owed him that much. Perhaps he would return the watch.

I settled on Australia. Mining, ranching, and construction. *There* was a place that required a man who understood how to procure things, a man with contacts and shipping know-how like me. I could get word to Henrietta on arrival.

At the docks, I purchased a berth on a steamer leaving that afternoon and spent the morning buying clean clothes and a suitcase. I'd arrive with fewer possessions than when I shipped out to war, yet, from what I had heard, Australia was a country where people started out with nothing more than fresh ideas for a better life. The old fortune-teller was right about my lucky escape, and now it was up to me to make the most of my last chance. I owed it to the people who weren't so fortunate that day.

Jeffrey Huang

My father and I used to stand at the rail, close to the finish line, but I was too nervous to watch this race. If my gamble came off, I could watch from the members' enclosure next time as an owner. If it didn't…

In order to avoid the screens, I entered the gift shop and studied the framed photographs of the track over the years. The area was different then — green hills and colonial outposts. A beautiful black and white print showed the racecourse before the fire. The stadium seemed so open, with just one wooden structure for spectators. Ladies with parasols and gentlemen in waistcoats completed the scene.

I can tell you the winning time of the race to the nearest hundredth, the jockey of each of the horses and the colours they wore that evening, but I didn't stand at the rail, cheering them on. Not without Jack.

When I heard the roar of the crowd, I knew the favourite had won. Born in China came home three lengths ahead, as expected, but I needed to know if my lucky number eight had got second. I dared not speak to anyone. My focus remained on the photographs until the heat of the crowd had died down, then I finally went to check the big screen. The ticket in my pocket was everything or nothing — the wedding that Vanessa deserved, or the end of my dream to play a part in this sport.

The screen was blank. Processing. I waited. The losing punters returned to their seats and switched their focus to the next race. Winners double-checked their tickets and started mentally spending the winnings. Finally, the result emerged. First was Born in China in a time of 1:09:11, second was number eight, House of Fun in 1:09:48. When I saw the number, energy blazed through my body. I clutched the rail and let out a war cry. I had done it!

The quinella payout was almost nine times what I'd bet. When the jockey brought the winner down the track for his victory lap, he was barely sweating although I was still clutching the rail. Deep breaths. The opium-warm glow of the evening.

After the jockeys weighed in and the result was confirmed, I headed to the grandstand. The pensioner wasn't there. He'd been swallowed up by the other thousands of racegoers. The uniformed betting clerk counted out my winnings patiently as I waited to stow it in my bag. With the final five hundred dollar note of my winnings, I returned to the gift shop for the black and white photograph of Happy Valley.

Wedding troubles sorted. Got the second installment. A text to Vanessa. I couldn't call. She would hear the crowds and the ecstacy in my voice. At the gate, I leafed through the racing section and sent another message. *Interest in the Captain Jack syndicate.* All the way home on the MTR, I clung to the bag as if it were my baby. The next day, I was the proud part-owner of a very good horse.

I've told the story to the syndicate so many times I've lost count. 'How could you risk everything?' they ask. They mock me and call me *Lucky Jeffrey*. I saw the path and followed the signs.

The picture hangs in our hall, a monument to my eternal bond with my father. Each time Captain Jack races, I tap the frame on the way out, in remembrance of the people who died. It helps keep my luck alive.

Peloton

When thousands of riderless bicycles appeared on the night of June 23rd, there was simply no room for cars on the road. East End streets once plagued by fumes and noise fell silent but for the mechanical whirring of gears running loose chains.

The bikes glided past the Stratford Velodrome, laying their invisible tracks, dancing left and right, the pedals turning of their own accord. Some were old and rusted, others were racing bikes. A few once belonged to children. There were no motors or hidden controls, no miraculous winds to power them. Nobody knew how they arrived, or what brought them into existence. They followed the contours of Queen Elizabeth Olympic Park, turning right through Bow, into Mile End, and down towards the Thames. Drivers waited and watched.

In the beginning, the bicycles caused chaos with their unpredictable movement. They travelled clockwise, around a huge circuit of streets, like they were competing in a race with no rules and no finishing line. Capturing and dismantling them didn't help, it just resulted in the appearance of an identical one the next morning, completing the herd of exactly eight thousand one hundred and twenty-eight machines. Each circuit, the group stuck together, piling into the Rotherhithe Tunnel and racing back over Tower Bridge. Both were shut.

Journalists came in droves, each reporting the same as the news crews next to them: Eight thousand 'ghost bikes'. The Council thought it best to close the affected area. Politicians and other interested parties searched for a solution. Traffic lights got reprogrammed.

Once the initial media interest calmed, the theories began to spread: the bikes were a stunt to promote green transport; they were a PR project designed to boost tourism; they were an art installation. According to some, they signalled the second coming of the saviour. And still, they rode the streets. Around they went.

They became celebrities. People tried to grab the bicycles and mount them, as if they were wild horses waiting to be broken, so the Government passed a hasty law which made it a criminal offence to interfere with them. The track never changed — past The Tower of London, left at Queen Mary University, and back to the velodrome, through Victoria Park. Hundreds of volunteer police formed a protective cordon. Each bicycle featured on a government website along with a personality quiz, 'Which ghost bike is yours?'

Statisticians and officials theorised. 8,128 is the fourth 'perfect number', but apart from that, they found nothing significant. They went through the traffic statistics, the route they took, the national archives, and even the religious texts. The official White Paper offered no satisfactory evidence.

Then, one by one, as they passed into the tunnel, the bicycles died off. At first, just a few disappeared, then the pace quickened. Residents of the city and people around the world mourned their disappearance like they were an endangered species. 'Save our cycles'. The cameras brought to track their every move showed that at midnight every night, the one in last position at the back of the group vanished.

In a few months, they were gone. The cordons were lifted and pedestrians tiptoed around the 'track', convinced they might return any moment. Soon, the government waved in the cars and the vans and the lorries back. Fumes rose, but businesses breathed a sigh of relief.

Now, once per year, on June 23rd, the roads are closed and cyclists ride the route in an organised celebration — The Peloton. Millions from around the world enter into a lottery draw for a place, and 8,128 lucky riders take part. Each participant is assigned a number and rides a replica of the original machine. They log data and photos on the website for all to see. The event is broadcast on national television and groups gather to watch at cycle-themed parties. While few people will ever get the chance to ride in The Peloton, millions hope the riderless bicycles will someday return.

The Idea of Eve

Jesus, this guilt. Twenty years later, and I still picture her during sex, how she looked up at me, stared into me, through me. It's become a battle to shout my wife's name rather than hers when we make love.

Tracy rolls over and kisses me deep. 'Happy Father's Day, love.'

It doesn't feel happy, but I put on my best grin. 'Thanks.' They say happiness is more than love and security. It's governed by rules outside my consciousness. They weren't outside Eve's consciousness.

I turn back to my side of the bed and close my eyes. Two hours, that's what I've promised myself, a nice lie-in. Daydreams aren't productive but lie-ins make you fresher. At the end of it, is that how we're judged? Were you productive?

Every milestone that goes by might somehow purge the memories of that brief relationship in 2001, but they only get stronger. I find myself smelling her hair, or tracing her smile in my mind's eye. It's become a perversion. Eve has become a silent partner in my marriage. Tracy doesn't know she exists, but she's noticed I'm distant, distracted. I'm rarely in the present where I'm supposed to be. Even at family wedding speeches, when I'm filming my boy's first steps, or cuddled up on the sofa with Tracy, Eve sits next to me, nonchalantly smoking a cigarette and passing the hours and minutes.

For me, failure is an everyday occurrence. Giving up on my marriage would be a failure. Eve never failed. She never had a relationship.

Back then, I was a skinny nineteen-year-old on a gap year, before media studies, before life. South America. Every country forced my eyes open another inch. Each sprawling city with millions of different faces, each click of my camera, each group of effortlessly cool travellers, each failure. Then Eve reset the rules for everything.

She first appeared in an internet café in Arequipa, Peru. Back in the early noughties travellers used to send round-robin emails to family and friends. While my photos uploaded, she came in and perched by the door. She formed part of the scene, deliberately put there — the subject of the photo and the eye of the lens all in one. The connection was so slow, she'd have to wait too, but she wasn't impatient, she just smoked and looked at the street. A curtain of blonde hair almost reached the plastic stool. She was around my age, but her face showed the maturity of a gallery portrait. She wore a look which was neither inquisitive nor bored, but neutral, like she already understood the world. Freckles dotted her straight nose. When she finished her cigarette, she flicked the butt onto the dusty street and lit another.

My photo upload progress creeped towards forty per cent. 'Can I bum a smoke?' I didn't even smoke.

She shrugged then flicked open the packet with her thumb. To offer me the cigarette, she tossed it up and caught it by the white end. 'Ze internet is a shit, no?'

'Yeah slow, right?' We studied each others' faces. Hers had symmetry and poise, the depth of her green eyes limitless. She had something essential about her — answers to my unknown questions. A glance at my watch. A thirty minute wait.

'Time is only an illusion.'

Was that a joke? 'What do you mean?'

'Well, it's 'ard to imagine time from ze perspective of another person.'

'Suppose it is hard.' No idea what she meant. To me, the progress of my photos, the internet, and the seconds spent in that conversation passed like days. When I coughed and spluttered on the harsh cigarette, she smirked. She didn't ask the usual travel questions and seemed allergic to offering information about herself. We gave the street cats names and invented a game where we tried to hit the empty juice cartons in the street with stones.

By the time my photos had uploaded, the game had about six sub-rules and a complicated point structure. She protested when she missed. 'No, it was in. *Putain*!'

We paid a couple of *soles* to the café owner and walked up the hill back towards my hostel.

'Ze view is incredible.'

Facing the cityscape, I really drank it in for the first time — white buildings set against the heavy mountain backdrop. That image is branded into my memory.

Eve lived in a homestay and worked in a local school, but she didn't elaborate. It was just something she did. My trip consisted of half-made decisions and fear of missing out. Eve had a perfect gauge when 'enough' strayed into 'too much'.

When we met in the internet café again, she accepted my invitation to the gringo hostel bar. She avoided the calls of a loud group of Aussies shovelling in burgers and making team lists for beer pong. You never forget that first out of body, out of place experience. Even now, around the table for dinner with my family, I sense someone else there.

That night we talked over the noise of clinking glasses and unmade travel plans. Lo-fi lounge music played in the background. Every ten minutes or so, she made a note in her book.

'What's that, a journal?'

'It's my little book. For stories.'

'What about?'

She paused. 'About ze things zat people do.'

Eve never used more words than were necessary, she saved them for better occasions.

In Cuzco, we slept together for the first time. I had followed her around like a puppy for a week and spent almost a month's budget on a private room. The sun shone into the room and the red curtains flapped in the breeze like an exotic perfume ad. When we got to it she didn't talk. No questions. The altitude made our hearts pound and our lungs burn. No amount of time, from anyone's perspective, could be enough. As we lay intertwined on the bed, I went to kiss her and she turned her head so it landed on her cheek.

Tracy says I have an addictive personality. It's usually my family who wants more. If it were up to me, I'd process life like Eve, not focus on 'being productive'. Back then, I hadn't learned the world isn't a meritocracy. Rooftop cocktails rested on tables high above the city where most people ate once a day.

Things feel real the first time you hold them, then you lose your sense of touch. For that first time, Eve was real. My mind raced forward through the life of our imagined relationship. Now it picks at the bones of the what-ifs and missed opportunities. Some days I saw her, and some days she avoided me. Every time I got tired of tracking her down, she would turn up and spend a day with me, giving me just enough encouragement to believe in the future I'd created. Eve never gave excuses and I never asked for them.

After Machu Picchu, we didn't see each other for a while. Hostel owners gave me that knowing look when I asked if they had seen a French girl with blonde hair who never said much. She probably read my emails in an internet café with a wry smile and a cigarette between her fingers.

The other week, one of the camera assistants offered me some of his joint and I refused. Memories of the stupid shit I did in Latin America came flooding back. When you're a father, you can't afford a moment of anti-sobriety. Drive the kids. Check the schedule. Tracy prints a spreadsheet every week. Does Eve still write things down in her notebook? With her, I'd have snorted quicklime if she'd suggested it. We spent weeks drifting through Peru and Bolivia, either high or coming down. We shared joints and drank beer for breakfast. She bought LSD in Puno and had perspective-changing visions at the lake. I spent three hours crying in a supermarket. She laughed when I told her I thought the cereal box mascots were plotting to kill me. One night in Sucre we hoovered spoons of coke in an unoccupied Police box. She gave me a blowjob. The tinted window shielded us from the pedestrian bodies a few feet away. My muscles wound so tight with energy I thought I'd burst through the wall and run with my pants down shouting *Viva Bolivia*. The weight fell off me. My camera shutter stopped clicking. My group emails waited. Catching a glimpse of the world through the eyes of Eve was all that mattered.

I've never felt that way about Tracy. The sex is constructive, like we're working together, building our little empire. Every time I wonder what the me in Eve's parallel universe might be doing, I jeopardise that empire. Maybe I'll forget Jonny's birthday, or that the bailiffs will break down the door. By clinging on to the rarified air of the Andes, the smells of markets and streets, the psychedelic visions, I risk missing the present. A change of scenery could work, and not just a caravan holiday to the Pembrokeshire coast — somewhere with jagged mountains and whole galaxies in the sky. The air in the bedroom smells stale and vaguely of sex. The air outside is grey.

Tracy bursts into the bedroom and interrupts my thoughts. She wants me to get out of bed even though my two hours isn't up. Jonny has blocked the toilet and is now crying. I make a tent with the covers and climb under.

'Seriously!' she says. 'Ten minutes.'

It doesn't matter that it's a Sunday, the messages will be non-stop, and I'll be organising the whole week before it's begun.

Time is sometimes like a montage — we experience the best bits, the worst bits. When stories go at the actual pace of life we lose the thread.

Not having a photo makes it all the more important to remember every detail of Eve. When I reached for my camera, she would put her hand over the lens and say 'photographs tell ze wrong story.' Pretty much our whole life is recorded now. It pays my bills. Without any pictures of Eve, the sound of her voice, her ticks, the cast of curtain-filtered light on her body, and the bones of her hand gripping a pen burn their image deep. The colours never lose lustre, their definition perfect. Time perfected my mental image, adding little brushstrokes every time I remembered some morsel of wisdom she tossed my way.

Some weeks later, we reached Uyuni, where the road ends and the salt flats start. My trip had a few weeks left and my funds had moved into the red. We shared the headphones from my iPod as the bus weaved through the hills. Short Bolivian women sat up straight, wrapped in colourful shawls. One earpiece each didn't drown out the jerky *cumbia* music.

'What are you going to do after all this?'

She looked at me and cocked her head. 'Zere is not an end for me, Angus.' She pronounced my name *on-goose.* 'Life is not a march towards death.' I hadn't suggested it was. 'You can think forward, so 'oo is to say ze present you, is not a memory from the future.'

Like always, I couldn't prove her wrong. Didn't she have somewhere to be? Where is she now? Probably a few steps ahead of some poor guy tagging along, trying to find the key that will unlock answers to the same questions I had. Reality is in some way malleable. There was never one true Eve.

Huts grew to buildings and the town came into view. Eve stared straight ahead. 'In Uyuni, I'm not coming wiz you.' Her voice held. Level. Matter of fact.

'What are you talking about?'

'Zere is a friend I 'ave in Uyuni. We go on motorbike.'

Eve had taught me to live in the moment, but I've ended up stuck in that one. My thoughts span. My stomach churned and my legs ached. The bus took an age to pull into the station. I said something petty like 'Well, what the fuck is the point of all this?'

She said something prophetic like 'Not everything 'as to 'ave a point. You will see, Angus.' I can't remember it exactly. Then we were quiet. We stared at the seats in front of us.

Uyuni. 12,000 metres above sea level. My sternum caved. Shallow breaths. I told her I thought I loved her. She didn't say anything to that. When she tried to kiss me goodbye and I turned my head so she kissed my cheek.

She suggested a drink at the Extreme Fun Pub later, but I didn't go. She walked away and the sun sank beyond the white horizon. I cried dry tears, same as I do after sex sometimes. Time ruptured in that moment and a part of me has been sitting on that rucksack for all of my adult life.

My trip ended in Argentina. Restaurant steak and unbranded red wine, cemetery tours and football matches in famous stadiums. My camera captured hundreds of pictures I've not looked at since. Friends asked if it changed my life. I shrugged and played it cool. That's what Eve would have done.

I haul myself out of bed and check my watch. By the time I've unblocked the toilet and answered my messages, it will be midday. Is it ever okay to wish away your obligations? Fill the sink with water. Sharpen the mind. I'll wash away my sins before Tracy and the kids can see them written on my face.

Moments are not linear. We live each one, but past versions of ourselves relive them again and again. A ghostly image of Eve's face appears in the bathroom mirror and she looks back at me. 'Angus,' she says, 'We always want what we can't 'ave. Human nature, no?'

Why do I keep going back over all this? I can't fall out of love with her ideas but I can let go of the *idea of her*. Maybe this will be the last time, the last time I take that bus journey with Eve. And yet, I know that the next time the kids are tucked up in bed, and there's an empty bottle of wine on the coffee table, I'll make love to my wife and I'll think of Eve. Then, the next morning, I'll perform this whole post mortem again.

Marbles and Memories

'The mind is a complicated thing, Mrs Spenmore.'

I sighed. 'Mine's a bloomin' mystery. That's the one thing I'm certain of.'

Mary didn't laugh. She was an unusually serious woman.

Misplacing things concerned me. A few weeks before, I'd found a red-lettered gas bill in the kitchen, a cheese and tomato sandwich going green in the conservatory, and a pair of Gerald's Christmas socks (red *and* green) hiding in the television cabinet. At least those things had turned up. I'd lost the keepsake I bought on our honeymoon — a little glass lighthouse filled with patterned sand from the Isle of Wight.

Mary peered over her sharp nose. Gerald called her 'the memory bird'. He wasn't wrong. She looked just like a bird — not Big Bird from Sesame Street, more like a startled crane. But, she was patient, and according to the classified section of the *Falmouth Packet*, there were no other qualified experts in the area.

'Stick to the process, Mrs Spenmore. You've made steady progress since we started.'

'I've told you, call me Maggie.'

Honestly, a 'memory retention consultant' should remember to call her clients by their first names. The whole 'Mr and Mrs' thing reminded me of my twenty-five years spent as secretary to a prickly lawyer, Herbert Blake. After a quarter of a century of service, he deemed it proper to send me a plain red Christmas card. *Dear Margaret, Happy Christmas, Mr Blake*.

'Here's the list,' she said, 'household objects, numbered. I'll give you a minute to create your narrative.' She'd conveniently forgotten the question about whether my memory was deteriorating.

Mary came once a week and we did mental exercises, recounting dreams and excavating details of life events, big and small. I could barely follow the reruns of Time Team that Gerald watched. What hope did I have of unearthing finds in my muddied memory?

That particular session, I wanted to better my record for memorising objects in order. One time I managed thirteen. No danger of getting past that unlucky number, let alone troubling the current world record holder Prejish Merlin, who had listed four hundred and seventy objects in order. Practise, practise, practise, Mary said, but she dodged my question about how many *she* could remember.

'The trick is to rhyme the number and include an object as part of the image in your mind's eye,' she said.

Rhymes never came easy to me. My literature form tutor once described my poems as infantile, which I personally thought was harsh criticism for a twelve-year-old.

Try again. 'Number one. Daz washing powder.'

One rhymes with son. I imagined Nicholas all those years ago before he moved to New Zealand with his boyfriend. He wore brilliant white underpants, not when he moved, but when I pictured him as a toddler. I'd always been loyal to the brand, even when *Which? Magazine* downgraded it to fourth best for stain removal. Nicholas's boyfriend is called Darren, but he isn't a Daz. Gerald turned a certain shade of beetroot when our son came out. Of course, I'd known for years. Mothers find things in their children's bedrooms, while fathers are organising the tool shed or shouting at rugby matches on the telly.

'Two. A bowl of *potpourri*.'

Two rhymes with new, as in 'new house'. We'd wanted to move for some time, but the market never worked in our favour. Gerald said viewings interrupted his circadian rhythms. At first, I thought he meant his six o'clock ablutions, but he said it means sleep patterns. The young families viewed our place as old-fashioned. What did they expect from a pair of pensioners, strobe lights in the kitchen and a solar-powered toilet? The estate agent sprayed an awful fragrance of baked cookies for that 'authentic homely smell'. Nothing beats the tried and tested scents. I love the smell of *potpourri* in the morning.

Mary reached down and brought the items onto the table as I identified them, like The Generation Game only in reverse. She's too young to have watched it in its heyday. Now, what was—?

'Three?' she said, interrupting my daydream about a young Bruce Forsyth.

Three sounds like tree, or at least an Irish person saying three. 'Ah yes,' I said, 'the Tai chi book.' I'd put the book up a cherry tree in my mental picture. Lionel Blair perched on the lowest branch, legs swinging, flicking through the book. He'd been at the opening of some assisted-living flats I viewed in Bridport, but I'd been too embarrassed to meet him. The follow-up sales call confused Gerald. 'We're not even seventy yet, Maggie,' he stammered. 'Those places are for fruitcakes and crones.'

Four was easy. Pussy Galore, the only woman I'd ever fancied. 'Playing cards.' Goldfinger was a nasty cheat, wasn't he?

Mary placed the cards with the other items.

Onwards to five. What rhymes with five. Jive? Beehive? Nosedive? External hard-drive? It didn't matter any more. The system had gone. I got lucky with Goldfinger, and thirteen was a long way off.

While I certainly didn't miss Mr Blake, I did miss work. Watching Eggheads on BBC Two every day didn't really count as an accomplishment. I'd even applied to go on the show with the ladies from Yoga. Mind, Body and Seoul we were called. Jessie was actually from Tai Wan, but she said she'd pretend to be Korean so we could use our clever team name. We would donate the prize to Dementia UK. Gerald and I had seen what the disease did to his mother.

Back in my kitchen, Mary watched me struggle. The hour ticked down, and she was about to do that thing where she slapped her legs and said 'right,' before upping and leaving.

'Six. Car keys,' I blurted, putting a stop to any thigh slapping. Six rhymes with Weetabix. The keys were hidden inside one of Gerald's bloody cereal boxes in my image. Two packets a week he got through. More than a thousand 'bix' per year. We could have built a second home out of all those wheaty bricks he's put away over the course of our marriage. He brought them with him on holiday, even on domestic trips. Even on our honeymoon in Ventnor. They say marriage is about sacrifice, well, I'd sacrificed plenty of space in the suitcase for his immoveable concept of breakfast over the years. Such a shame we hadn't been back to the Isle of Wight.

A hand touched my arm. 'Mrs Spenmore? Maggie? Where've you gone?'

It must have been a full thirty seconds since my last word. 'Sorry… just thinking about breakfast.' I must've sounded ridiculous.

'Everybody's thought patterns are different,' she said, wearing the same sympathetic look as the doctor who admitted a three-year-old me to A&E after I ate plasticine. 'Sorry, our time is up.'

Something about those words pressed a button that shouldn't be pressed — a big red button with a protective case over it. I was alarmed. My time was

57

up. Before long, I'd forget the stories behind all of these objects. My mind would become a rusty law-office filing cabinet, pushed off a cliff by a maniacally laughing Mr Blake. Lionel Blair would watch from his tree.

Mary gathered her things. 'Now,' she said, 'I'll be away for the next two weeks. Remember I'm off to Ireland for a conference. Tipperary.' It might as well have been Timbuktu.

As soon as the door closed, my lost key fob sprang to mind. I was normally so careful with things. We had an organisation system for my tea towels even though we only had three. My time was up. The well inside me rose. I sat on the stairs and sobbed. That was the first time I'd cried since Nadiya won the Bake-Off finale, and no one can begrudge tears for such an emotional moment. Blobs of salty water squeezed through the gaps in my fingers, over my hands and onto the carpet.

Gerald found me a few minutes later. 'What's the memory bird said to you, love?' His face was blurry through the tears. His hair slicked into a side parting like he was a child off to a birthday party. He stood back a foot or two, calculating the severity of my latest 'Maggie moment'.

'Oh, don't worry, love. Just losing my marbles is all.'

'Just as long as you've not lost your marbles,' he said, pretending not to hear me. He always could cheer me up with his silliness. 'Memory class not go well?' he asked, sitting next to me on the bottom step of the stairs.

I dried my eyes. 'Can't think where I could have lost that key fob. You know, the one with—'

'You mean this?' He held up the glass lighthouse.

I gasped. 'But it's empty.'

'Mary got you doing observation as well? Nothing gets past you.'

'Where did you find it?'

'Well, I've got a confession to make, love.' Now he definitely looked like a naughty schoolboy. 'You know I misplace my car keys on occasion?'

I did know. I'd threatened to get him one of those elastic keychains to clip to his jeans.

'I err… borrowed yours last week, dropped them in the supermarket car park and it—, well, the sand came out. Tried to catch it with my foot to cushion the impact, but I just ended up drop-kicking it into this woman's trolley.'

Was I relieved or angry? At least I'd stopped crying.

'She was asking the trolley-collector bloke for help and didn't see it go into her shopping. Let me tell you, she did not appreciate me rummaging through her groceries. The poor thing was eighty-odd and rammed me with her trolley to get me to stop. Must have thought I was after her fondant fancies or something.' Gerald continued without taking a breath as I listened in amazement. 'I had to explain to the trolley warden why there was coloured sand leaking into this woman's shopping. I told him to be careful, but he plunged his hand in and cut himself on the thing.'

That made me wince.

'Luckily, the woman had bought some plasters for her granddaughter and patched him up with a pink Hello Kitty bandaid.'

I was crying again, but this time with laughter. He chuckled and said it was a wonder the police weren't called. It took me a good minute to compose myself. 'I can just imagine it, you daft sod.'

'Sorry. It's important to you, so…' Gerald handed me the glass trinket. 'I wanted to fix it first.'

The glue held it together so well, you'd never know it was broken. 'Shame it's empty,' I said.

He said we could fill it up when we go.

'Go where?'

He beamed. 'The Needles of course. I've booked us WightLink ferry tickets and a couple of nights in a B&B in Ventnor.'

There I was cursing his Weetabix, and he'd gone and done something so romantic. 'Is it the same one?'

'God no,' he said, 'health inspectors closed it down years ago.'

Gerald got to his feet, but he was two steps further up, so when I went in for a kiss my head met the level of his bulging stomach.

'That's not all,' continued the belly. 'I've booked an appointment with an estate agent. You've always loved it there, and we might get more for our money.'

Views out into the English Channel, the breeze in my hair, walks along the cliffs. 'Marvellous,' I said.

'Better than those retirement flats.' I went into the kitchen, put the key fob on the kitchen table along with the other items, and switched the kettle on. 'What about your rugby club, love?'

He shrugged. We needed a change of scenery.

'And I won't miss any classes with Mary. She's off to Tipperary. Probably come back a nun.'

'Sister Mary Magpie?'

We laughed.

The kettle boiled and Gerald poured the tea. 'Now you've learned her secrets, you could fly the nest, set out on your own.'

We sat at the table and an item brushed against my foot. There were still a good few objects under there. Gerald reached down to clear the space for our legs but I stopped him. 'Wait.' I looked around the room, with its 1980s tiles, pine chairs and oversized radio. We'd been in the place forty years, but the thought of a new house excited me. 'Let me try and finish my list.'

Gerald smiled. 'Go on then.'

'Seven… pen. Eight… err, thimble. Nine… pine… our framed photo.'

Gerald rummaged under the table and pulled out the corresponding items. Like shooting ducks in a barrel. No, wait. Ducks in a row. *Fish* in a barrel.

'Ten, now that's *um*, a baseball cap. Eleven… Radio Times Magazine. That's it. Now, twelve… Banana!' How had I done that? The images in my mind lined up like a very respectful set of suspected

61

criminals. 'Thirteen, green... plants. Oh, the packet of tomato seeds.'

Gerald grinned and held up a finger. 'One more, love.'

Was the curse of thirteen about to be lifted? Fourteen... Mr Bean, Vaseline, amphetamine, Come on Eileen, dialysis machine, poly-tetra-fluoroethylene? I was in one of those spirals again, trapped in a cycle of rhyming memories. Gerald got up to busy himself in the kitchen. Then it hit me. *Bright sheen.* 'A pack of glass marbles.' (Well, they were decorative glass beads really, but Gerald would appreciate the joke.)

'*Yes*. Well done, my love.'

Fourteen in a row. I mean, Prejish Merlin had absolutely nothing to worry about, but my memory was improving, not fading.

'You did it,' said Gerald triumphantly, putting the dish of shiny glass beads onto the table.

I leaned back like the cat that got the cream. And I *did* get the cream because Gerald plated up two chocolate eclairs from the fridge while I *ummed* and *ahhed* over the last item.

'You'll be setting up shop in Ventnor next.'

'What do you mean?'

'Could be a good way to meet people. Take what you've learned from Mary, and offer some free classes. Nursing homes and the like.'

The idea of it. Me, the ageing memory mistress. Sipping my tea, I considered it all, a new place, and a new job. We might even run into elderly celebrities like Lionel Blair.

'Come on,' said Gerald, pointing to the telly. 'Eggheads is about to start.'

The Quiet Cosmonaut

Be glorious, our free Motherland
A reliable stronghold of the peoples' friendship!
Banner of the Soviets, banner of the people,
May it lead from victory to victory!

The lyrics make my chest swell. You must always sing the anthem. Take a breath, open wide and belt out the words. Of course, no sound escapes. It never does. I have no voice. In spite of this, it's down to me to prove that greatness and communism are inseparable. In three minutes, I'll open the highway to the stars for Russia.

I climb into the small vessel. The flight module has the appearance of a deep sea diving helmet, only big enough for one occupant. Once inside, my mind enters its composed state and travels to a special place: Planet Quiet. To get there I block external sounds and smells and focus within. Deep concentration on the rhythmic beat of my heart and breathing. I carry out orders with efficiency and precision. This is the attitude a cosmonaut must demonstrate. My silence contains strength; it heightens my other senses.

Helmet attached, I fasten the pilot's seat straps. They must be secured, the same way every instrument in the Vostok 3KA was precision designed and fitted. Although I'm on my own from here, I am not alone.

The voice in my radio earpiece chimes like a school bell. 'Colonel Berezutski, final systems check.'

RCS and main engine pressure gauges, electrical systems and battery charge — readings relayed quicker than any others can. Morse code from the transmitter next to my right leg is instantly decoded by Russian Mission Control Centre in Korolyov. The countdown drones away in my earpiece. I await further instruction.

Grigori Berezutski on the cusp of pioneering space travel and becoming a leader of the people. Back in Omsk, Father will be proud. My distinguished military career will bring good fortune to the collective farm this year. Mother will toast my success with her friends. Yet, my biggest driving force has been not been the support of my family, but that of *Grigori gluppy*, or 'Stupid Gregory', once a favourite taunt of those at school. Then, the Young Pioneers who tried to draw audible sounds with their fists, and later the measured silences of the other Air Force pilots. They have made me this way: stoic for the Motherland.

As the countdown sequence approaches one minute, the voice at RMCC comes back to life. 'Berezutski, fire alarm, sector 7D. Report.'

A red light flashes and my mind skips forward three moves. If it's overheating, it will be a simple solution: employ the thermo-negative coolant. But, if there's a fire…

'Code 98, Berezutski. Urgent. Report before T-minus ten.' The normally steady lieutenant's voice cracks over the radio. The whole launch is in jeopardy. My hands tear off the canvas restraints and I roll out of the chair to face the fire. No smell of combustion, but experience tells me the blaze could be coming from within the Vostok launch vehicle, housed between the unpressurized compartments of the reentry shell. My internal metronome estimates fifty-two seconds. *Stay calm, Colonel Grigori.*

When I rip off the control panel, the pressure remains constant. No blast of heat enters the module. No compromise. *Return the panel and turn the pressure clamps, Grigori.* Forty seconds. The SK-1 suit stifles manoeuvre. When reindeers fight against the farmer's rope, they find energy from deep. They struggle. They buck and pull for minutes, not seconds. To have any chance of mission success, I must return to the seat and deactivate the alarm. *Fight.* Twenty-five seconds.

Mission control maintains stone silence. Frantic fingers flip combinations of switches on the control panel. Then an engine reboot. A searing bead of sweat runs the track of my spine. Inside my spacesuit, neck muscles tighten. The clock ticks to fifteen. Perspiration from my heightened breathing steams my visor.

The warning light still flashes. I cast my mind back to Command Officer Nizkhin's lecture on logic gates — two negatives can create a false positive. I will not allow this launch to be postponed. Twelve seconds. Is it too late to save the mission? I reach forward and depress the cabin overheat button. Eyes closed. Breathe.

'... False alarm signal, Berezutski. Mission proceeds in 10... 9... 8,' says the voice with relief. Sometimes, even hi-tech electronic computer circuits can be outmanoeuvred.

Back in position, I squint through the front porthole. Opaque grey sky awaits. Wind speed is stable and the rain clouds will hold. Five seconds to launch. My muscles tense, anticipating the force that will slowly build to 9Gs. After hundreds of flight hours and simulations, operations are muscle memory, but, keeping your body and mind together under such stress takes a special energy. Planet Quiet.

'3... 2... 1...'

The engines fire with a furious burst of power. The small craft rumbles and finally inches off the ground toward the atmosphere, toward its orbit of 177 km by 471 km with 64.9 degrees of inclination. Toward history.

'Grigori Berezutski!'

Another emergency. What could it be this time? Perhaps a ground technician has seen something. Trajectory issues?

'Stand up this instant.'

The tone is sharp. Such commands cannot be ignored. I unfasten my harness and get to my feet. My back hunches under the cabin roof.

'What on Earth are you doing? Don't you know it's going to rain?'

My spacecraft begins to disintegrate around me. The Vostok 8K72K launch vehicle drops away, hurtling earthward. Next, the RCS propulsion tanks explode — *boom*, *boom*! Finally, the module walls buckle and peel away leaving me exposed to the cool Omsk air.

I motion the outline of my helmet and point to the sky. *One day, I'll be a cosmonaut.*

She laughs. 'The dumb can't be cosmonauts, Grigori. Now get inside before you get that Young Pioneers uniform even muddier.'

Mother has interrupted another mission. The control panel in front of me fades and she towers over me with her arms folded across her good apron.

Why do they neglect me? Not one of the other Pioneers wanted to come and play. They went to Sasha Andropov's house because his father is a party official and has a wireless system with dual sound. Tears swell.

Mother smacks the dust off my shorts where the vibrations of the launch have caused stains. She ignores my protests and pushes me inside. Sometimes I think she blames me for the death of my twin sister. 'At least they could cry,' she once said.

Papa sits inside. He sprawls in the big chair, boots off. 'Grisha, my boy. Ready for the broadcast?' He fiddles with the knobs on the old radio. 'It will be magnificent.' Then, he grips my shoulders as if testing

69

the ripeness of a pumpkin. The skin on his hands is calloused and worn.

'Don't touch him, Vladimir,' says Mother. 'He's been rolling around in the mud like a stray dog.' Papa responds with a resigned nod.

Today was supposed to be a celebration. Mother opened a can of meat to eat with pickles and I hoped Papa would fill three cups of vodka instead of two this time. But, Mother's discontent hangs heavy, dominating the room.

The radio crackles into life and I'm transported back to RMCC.

—*Young cosmonaut Yuri Gagarin, prepares to achieve a great victory for the Soviet Nation. Conditions have been approved and the launch will commence at 1600 hours—*

First, they play the national anthem. Father stands and we all hold hands.

'Be glorious, our free Motherland. A reliable stronghold of the peoples' friendship!'

Determined to join in, I try to mouth the words, but the sounds that emerge are broken and deformed.

Mother turns down the volume on the wireless as the second verse arrives. She releases my hand and glares. 'Grigori. Do not use that ugly voice. How dare you disrespect the anthem. Shut up.'

Slowly, my mouth closes in defeat. My gaze reverts to the floor.

Mother looks at Papa until he understands the order and he slaps the back of my head. 'If God had wanted you to talk, he'd have given you a tongue,' she says. Then, she measures two more vodkas for her and Papa and dials the volume back up.

Another proud moment ruined. I turn to leave but she catches my arm. 'And don't think I haven't seen the stains on that shirt, Grigori. You'll pay for that with the belt.'

I squirm from her grasp and squeeze past her, heading for the safety of my pilot's seat before it's too late. Papa is slow, and misses me. I make it to the door, pull it open and run out into the rain.

The Omsk sky casts dark, and big rain droplets crash down to Earth. My legs carry me out of the gate and past the Mokhnatkin farm. Soon my white shirt slicks with rain and sticks to my skin. After a minute, I take refuge under a group of fir trees and catch my breath.

All you can ever wish for is the strength to become a Soviet hero. Planet Quiet can be a lonely place, yet no more lonely than my life at home. As soon as I'm strong enough, I vow to leave this place.

My internal metronome tells me that the launch will start in ten seconds. I march out to the muddy track and hold my finger in the air to determine the direction of Korolyov.

The sky punishes me by pouring unbroken torrents of tears. It is a fight to keep my eyes open. 'You can do it, Yuri! Make Russia proud!' I shout into the rain, again and again, filling my lungs and straining the muscles in my chest. No sound comes out.

Don Pedro's Dog

Winter

Down below, the *plaza* bristles with morning life. A stiff wind corals the last of the leaves, clearing the carpet of interlocking bricks underneath. People go about their business here, regardless of the conditions. We're not all mouth and no trousers, like they are down in Andalucía. I'll visit the library today, and make progress with my family research.

Life in the square gives me a sense of routine. Parents deposit mitten-handed schoolchildren and the snaking queue for the warmth of the medical centre grows. I sip my coffee out on the balcony, even though it's four degrees.

He's late today, the gentleman with the hat and the dog. Every day at ten, he walks the dog and takes in every inch of the square.

I've asked around, in a casual manner, trying not to alert the *abuelitas* in the block to the possibility of 'widow's gossip'. He's a little older, but he holds himself well. He dresses well, too.

Winter's no time for introductions, even if his dog is the perfect ice-breaker even for a shy type like me. Two months ago I lost *Blanquita*, my own four-legged companion. The flat feels cold without her. I used to fill her bowl with biscuits as the coffee pot boiled. Now I just stare out of the window.

My son, José, owns a Labrador, but they're not the same. Bigger dogs don't have the sharp personalities of the miniatures. He tells me to get a new pet. '*Mamá*, you need the company, and it will get you out of the apartment.'

Spring

These last months have seen my family tree sprout little shoots of hope. José took me to the cemetery in Guadalajara and the municipal archives in Soria. We unearthed a good number of dates, photos and even contact information for some distant cousins. When you ask the right questions in the right place, these new connections come in bursts.

The fixtures in the square are less consistent. Shops come and go before you get the chance to forge a relationship with them. A *Chino* family took over the café. I watch their children run between the stainless steel chairs in a game of 'you can't catch me'. Today I'll visit their café, read the paper, and try their *menu del día.*

The sun's high rays bathe the white buildings. A breeze drifts over from the mountains. Down below, a gypsy with a thick moustache idles while he delivers fruit to the shop. Nobody rushes their business here, not even delivery men.

Finally, he arrives. Don Pedro. That's the name I have given him, even though we've not spoken. He wears a diamond-patterned jacket, pressed grey trousers, and a short brimmed hat. With the lead in one hand and a cane in the other, he navigates the central garden of the square, taking shorter paces with his stiffer left leg. His sidekick, the overweight Chihuahua, hurries along behind him.

He's the one thing in this picture that won't be gone next month or even next year. I imagine he used to be a tradesman, something practical. Perhaps he has a gaggle of daughters who nag him to eat healthily. He likes to dance.

My coffee is cold. Some days I don't know where time goes. The dog sniffs the bushes and urinates on each post he passes. His owner completes three laps of the gardens, buys a lottery ticket from the kiosk next to the main road, and then smokes his pipe.

Sometimes he buys a *pintxo de tortilla* and eats it standing outside. He doesn't seem the type to dedicate himself to neighbourhood gossip. We're alike in that respect. I prefer to listen, and observe town life — the clinks of glasses, the movements of families heading to church, and the changing of colours as the warmer weather approaches. Is this what Don Pedro thinks about behind his tinted glasses and pipe smoke? My hand lifts in goodbye as he departs for another day. I head back inside to my books.

The clouds keep the sun at arm's length, but there's no breeze to speak of. These temperatures make everyone tired. While the school is out, nothing in the square moves.

He's late again today. Ten-fifteen comes and goes.

Last week I took the train to Madrid and visited the national archives. The documents I obtained informed me that some of the Garcías worked in Equatorial Guinea. Africa of all places. I suppose there's not much difference in temperature at the moment. Today I'll write to the addresses I found, then wait to see if anybody writes back.

Despite the hot sun, I wish the clouds away. They make me uneasy. The fruit gypsy has been replaced by a woman with a fringe and a tracksuit. Cars belch thick traffic fumes and the buses hiss as they come to a halt. Few passengers in August. Younger families have headed to the coasts of Cantabria or Galícia.

When Don Pedro shuffles into view, he clutches his stick in his left hand and his pipe in the right. The dog isn't with him. He wears a jacket and a black tie. In *this* heat? It would be terrible if his dog is unwell... or even worse. It's one friend after the other now, monthly trips to the cemetery for funerals.

Down below, the man completes his circuits of the square, smoking all the while, something on his mind. He stops and inspects every corner of the space, walking the routes his Chihuahua did the days and months before. The vendor in the lottery booth perks up as he passes, but Don Pedro neglects to buy a ticket.

As he taps the pipe tobacco into the bin, he catches me watching. He looks right at me. The embarrassment. I don't want to be seen as one of those loud-mouthed grandmothers who have nothing better to do than spy on others all day. I have my family, my books, my research. Just as I lower my gaze to pretend I was watching something else, the man waves up at me and smiles. He *has* noticed. We have our own patterns and routines, and today, I'm part of his. We are the two constants of this ever-changing *barrio*. I wave back sympathetically, hoping that the black tie doesn't mean what I think it means.

Autumn

The forecast was for cool weather, but when I pull back the curtains to the balcony the square is bright, as if someone adjusted the colour settings on my television screen.

As I step out, a warm breeze and the scent of roasting chestnuts greets me. The vendors have started their season. At the school gates, children whizz around as parents try to hand them lunch boxes and other forgotten items.

The fruit shop opens its shutters to reveal a display of beautiful red cherries. Everything's in balance, the *barrio* back to normal. Businessmen in suits drink their morning *café con leches* while reading the papers. Today I'll walk the city ramparts then along the river, where I used to go with *Blanquita*.

As I take a final glance at my surroundings, I notice a familiar figure entering into the picture. Although he's been absent this last month, he's early today, wearing his familiar green jacket and walking at a brisk pace. He turns into the *plaza* and as he does, a sand-coloured ball of fur scurries past him and into the garden. The dog is back, and better than ever. God bless the little thing. A healing smile forms.

Without giving it a second thought, I take the elevator down, and step out into the square.

Don Pedro calls his dog. '*Vaya, Arturito. Haz tu negocios allí.*' I chuckle to myself. Of course, the dog is called Arturo; the same as my fat little ex-husband. What a wonderful coincidence.

'Excuse me, sir.'

He removes the pipe from his mouth. 'Oh hello. You live on the block, no?'

'Yes.' I feel like the nervous teens I see outside the school. 'I've a question about your dog.'

'Arturo? He's been poorly.'

'Yes, I gather. It's been a year, since my… well, I was considering a Chihuahua and just wondered about—'

'Oh, they're wonderful.' His face brims with the energy of a much younger man. 'My son breeds them.'

I laugh at the thought of his family around the dinner table each with a tiny dog in tow.

Don Pedro says, 'Here, take this.'

The business card reads Jose Calleja Vasquez Jr. So he is actually Don Pepe Snr. I was so close.

'I really am interested,' I say. 'I'd like a new dog soon, before winter.'

'Best to get things organised,' he says.

There's never the perfect time for new beginnings, but each autumn feels like it's my last chance to start something. Years go by. We share a glance, an understanding. 'I'd love to chat more. To get more information,' I say.

Arturo interrupts our moment by pulling at the lead.

'He's an impatient old mutt, like me,' he says. 'When he has to go…'

'I understand,' I say.

'*Encantado.*' He tips his hat, as gentlemen have done for generations, and with that, they're gone. I feel a rush, like I do when I discover an old relative's name. Another piece of the puzzle completed. Don Pepe.

Does he believe, like me, that things occur in cycles in this town? The square will still be here tomorrow, as will its occupants. In time, I will walk my new dog with Pepe and Arturo, and I hope that we will become part of this scene, for many seasons to come.

Consuming Life

Each Yoga class cost Sarah nearly one hundred Dirham, even if she went twice a week. Thirty dollars an hour. She pictured Arnold's look of disapproval at her indulgence, but keeping in shape made her feel better about living in a construction-kit city surrounded by desert. Sarah couldn't run in the evening heat like her boyfriend.

She stole a glance in the mirrored walls of the all-women fitness club. Most of the other members were in much worse shape than she was. It wasn't their fault; some Arabian women barely got out of the house. The instructor corrected their poses and cooed praise. She ignored Sarah.

What could it cost to rent the space, provide mats, and employ one teacher? The fees were outrageous, let alone the books, leggings and the equipment she bought. Sarah could afford it, but that wasn't the point. Arnold scrutinized every dollar and dime that left their joint account. Yoga, it seemed, was good business. Everyone in The Emirates clamoured for wealth and status. What happened to earning success little by little?

'Thank you, everybody. That's the end of the class for today.' The petite woman clasped her hands in a show of respect to the business magnates' wives in the room. Sarah gathered her gym pass, towel and bottle, and prepared to leave.

'Miss Sarah.' A familiar voice.

Sarah turned. Her colleague from The Four Seasons sported expensive-looking workout gear. Mansour didn't consider the price of anything much — her father was a big deal at one of the banks and her 'career' in hospitality didn't have much more time to run.

She liked Mansour, but got tired of deflecting invites to her family gatherings. An American marketing manager accepting her invitation would look very good. Sarah put on her customer-service voice. 'How did you find the class?'

Mansour laughed. 'Oh, very difficult, but I try to improve myself.'

Sarah agreed, her mind half occupied with the question of what Arnold would pick up dinner on the way home. Perhaps he would be in one of his cooking moods. 'Sure. Listen I've got—'

'I want to ask if you will come to my event at the hotel.' She brought up an advert on her Swarovski-bejewelled phone. It promised high-quality gift bags and a chance to meet the creator of Platinum Cosmetics.

'Mansour, I don't think I can. I know you worked hard to put this together, but I have plans.'

That was a lie. Arnold would be playing golf with clients on the weekend. Besides, Sarah knew enough about finance to spot a dressed-up Multi-Level

Marketing pitch when she saw one. The magazines she advertised The Four Seasons in were full of information about how Platinum Cosmetics could help you unlock your potential and attain the life of your dreams. 'I'll see if I can come... but no promises.'

Mansour raised onto tiptoes. 'Oh, good. Very good. It is a wonderful opportunity. You will see.'

That was also a lie. There would be judgemental mothers in burqas and beady-eyed chaperones watching on. Sarah wondered how many boxes of that junk Mansour had stored in her father's garage.

Sarah anticipated the cool shower in her sparse apartment, rinsing off the grime of the city. Neither Dubai nor Connecticut really felt like home anymore. Sarah missed the luxuries of restaurant quality food, glossy magazines, and the joy package deliveries. Emirati women shoved their wealth in your face — the watches, bags, crystal-studded gadgets. In Dubai Sarah felt plain and invisible.

Mansour left with a wave, probably off to buy her fruit smoothie and a copy of Cosmopolitan Middle East. 'See you at the hotel tomorrow,' she said.

At home, Sarah took a shower and put on one of her 'liberated' hotel robes. The apartment still looked bare after two years there. She filled the washing machine with her gym clothes but waited to start the cycle. Arnold might have something to add. Other couples had a maid, but her boyfriend was dead against it.

'We've got no children to look after, babe, and we need to save every penny for the plan.'

Sometimes she cursed that 'life plan' of his — Financial Independence, Retire Early — like life was all about beating the system. Arnold treated it as some kind of religion. He ran this kind of double life, pretending to value French food and seven-star hotels while eating rice and beans at home. He only cared about stocks in order to manage his own personal F.I.R.E. fund. He tried to get Sarah interested in the strategies and price-tracking data, but she preferred tangible investments. If they bought jewellery, property or art, at least she could enjoy the experience of looking at them.

Sarah made a mental note to buy more detergent and checked the monthly budget on the spreadsheet. It showed a healthy profit, despite a few lunchtime jaunts to the mall. She never bought much. Her retail therapy involved looking through the glass at the rows of organized rails and assistants with painted-on smiles. Having to walk away empty-handed was a bit like sex without a climax. Sarah never thought it would be this hard to live among luxury without touching any of the exhibits.

She remembered the 'conversations' about moving, which were really just sales pitches about the 'life plan' from Arnold. 'Do you think we could scrap *this* as our dream?' he had asked, brandishing a wedding magazine.

Sarah had flushed red. She *didn't* only care about material things but she loved seeing how happy the people in those pictures were. It was nice to desire things and feel the accomplishment of getting them. That's what the American education system taught you: how to *want* and how to *obtain*. In their Dubai apartment, they didn't even have a damned coffee table for magazines.

Sarah ordered some Indian take-out on the app. She missed tipping the pizza guys and seeing them thankful. In America, people still valued cash. Value in Dubai was determined by the type of car you drove and the number of staff you employed.

While she waited for the food, Sarah flicked through a few brochures she'd picked up at work. Even on short journeys, she liked to look through the in-flight magazines. They were pure escapism, but that was okay. Didn't everybody secretly dream of spa treatments and exclusive resorts? Maybe everyone except for her boyfriend, who used the time to study his financial plans.

In one of the magazines, Sarah came across an interview with a familiar face. She shifted herself to an upright position on the sofa. Becky Ferguson, one of her dorm-mates at Columbia, had a full page spread in Emirates magazine. The photo showed her in an exercise studio looking out onto a sunny pine forest. She wore a headband and clasped her hands in the *namaste* pose.

In the interview, Becky explained how her upstate New York project had been funded by just four years working in the city. According to the article, the average American spends $140 per day across seventeen transactions. Tall Pines sought to reduce that number to zero, and instil a culture of making and sharing. The title read 'Minimal Millennials'. Could she be happy with this lifestyle after the rollercoaster ride of working on Wall Street? Sarah made a mental note to reach out to her.

Just then, Sarah heard Arnold's key in the door.

'Woo, hot one.'

Sarah caught a glimpse of his damp blue shirt as he scurried into the bedroom to change. His black hair glistened with sweat.

'How was your day?' he asked from the room.

'All right, I guess. Went to Yoga. Got Indian for dinner.'

He shouted back, 'Babe, we've got to get used to cooking. I told you.'

It wasn't worth a fight. It was fifteen dollars. The ingredients would probably have cost the same in a supermarket. Sarah dropped the magazine onto the space where there should have been a coffee table. It slapped onto the tiled floor. She looked through the window at the night drawing in. 'Mansour asked me to go to her makeup event.'

Arnold shed his shirt and trousers and pointed his naked torso towards the AC. Even at nine PM, it was sweltering. 'That girl and those crappy MLMs.'

'She's just trying to be successful. It isn't easy here for women if you hadn't noticed.'

He put his hands on his hips. 'You're not going to go are you?'

Sarah promised she wouldn't. Her mind flashed forward to another weekend of television in their white cell compound, while Arnold sipped lemonade and shook hands at the golf club. 'It's just, it costs money to do *anything* here. I don't know how long I can—'

'Six months,' Arnold interrupted. 'When I get my bonus, we'll call it.'

'That's what you said last year.'

For a few seconds, the hum of the air conditioning unit did its best to fill space in the apartment.

Sarah decided to change the subject. 'Look at this.' She picked up the Emirates magazine and found the page with Becky Ferguson. 'This friend of mine from college is running a Yoga retreat.'

Arnold cast his eye over the article, his blue eyes flickering with calculations, projections and annual estimates. 'Huh.'

'Becky was never the type to preach minimalism. She was laser-focused on a law career.'

'Huh,' he said again. 'Guess we're all trying to get a little piece of freedom.' Arnold handed back the magazine like he was relinquishing responsibility for her friend's life. That's what Sarah hated about this 'retire early' idea. It cut you off from the world as if you were building a shelter and hiding from civilization.

Sarah's phone sounded with a message from Mansour.

My father is playing golf with Arnold tomorrow. How fantastic. You will come to the Platinum event? It can make such a difference.

Sarah sighed. She'd have to go now. Mansour craved recognition more than financial success, and supporting someone trying to make it on her own was the right thing to do.

Arnold took a bottle of water from the fridge and gulped it down in one. He refilled it from the tap and replaced it. 'Going for a run,' he said, and then went to pull on a pair of shorts and his sneakers. Of course, he wouldn't spring for a gym membership, he went running through the dusty air, past endless gray concrete.

'Wait.'

He asked what it was, as if he didn't know.

'How much is enough?'

Arnold stared back with a puzzled-labrador look on his face.

Sarah continued. 'We've made over a million dollars since we've been here.' It sounded ridiculous to say it out loud. *One million dollars.* 'When are we going to start building a life, not just a portfolio? I don't even know what home means anymore.' She stood up and motioned to the empty space in front of the couch. 'We don't even have a goddamn coffee table to put our stuff on.'

Arnold looked at the door. He had been so close to escaping. 'We don't drink coffee…'

Sarah glared, daring him to use his line about coffee being an overpriced cup of beans when he had a six-figure bonus cheque coming. 'Maybe I'll start,' she said. 'I'll get myself hooked so we can finally get a table for this room.'

He puffed out his cheeks.

Sarah knew what he was thinking. He was searching for some anti-capitalist statistic about how a barista might deal with hundreds of purchases in one day, and how that would keep them on the transaction treadmill for life. 'We're not saving to build a nuclear bunker,' she said with a sweeping hand gesture.

'All right. I know… I *know*.' He put a muscular arm around her shoulder. 'We'll talk when I'm back, okay?'

He always did that to diffuse the tension. As he left the apartment, he looked back and flashed a smile.

She seethed. Six more months. Then what? Even though she didn't drink coffee, western-style cafes were about the only places she found attractive in Dubai — friendly customer service, WiFi, beautiful cakes and cool A/C. Who didn't want that? Coffee was just a by-word for the social currency that was missing from her life. Cups normally came in twos and sat next to the magazines, on a little table next to luxurious chairs. The door buzzer interrupted her thoughts. Food delivery.

While she ate her portion of spiced rice and lentils, she thought of herself cooking meals in a farmhouse kitchen. Perhaps she would start a blog about using the produce they planned to grow on their land. That would make her college friends laugh. That figure of a million dollars bounced around her head.

Would it seem so enormous when there were extra mouths to feed?

For Arnold, this frugal life was freedom, but for Sarah, it just seemed like she was trading one kind of slavery for another. They both liked the idea of creating something together and building a family, but having it all at once seemed like cheating. And how would they explain it to her parents in Connecticut? They'd want to dote on their grandchildren, not chase them around a farmyard. They'd want them to go to the best private schools. Sarah's parents were the kind of people who had scaled life like a ladder, getting more and more careful as they climbed.

She must be missing something — the off-grid, back-to-basics lifestyle must be rewarding in ways she didn't understand. She got her tablet and searched for Tall Pines Community. Sure enough, Becky Ferguson's face beamed back from the homepage. According to the site, bookings were temporarily disabled. A further search of the internet revealed some negative reviews of the business and an entire thread on an NY Yoga forum discussing what had happened. Becky's partner had left, and she couldn't manage the place on her own. As of last month, the community had folded and the bank had foreclosed on the property.

Sarah nearly choked on her dinner.

A tearful post by Becky said she felt duped. It had been him driving the project, but when business took a downturn he left her with all the debt. Sarah wondered if Arnold had somehow guessed the business wasn't viable.

After finishing her meal, Sarah rested on the lumpy couch. She scrolled through the Ikea website and found a faux-walnut coffee table for under two hundred dollars. It was like the ones the Four Seasons had in their standard rooms, certainly not extravagant. She entered her credit card details on the screen and clicked the purchase button. As she did, that familiar hit of dopamine kicked in and she breathed a sigh of contentment. It would be even better when the thing arrived.

Each purchase decision from now on was going to be a big one, but she would stand up for herself more. They would acquire the life they desired, piece by piece. In the meantime, she'd have to deal with self-important Sheiks and trumped-up business events. Sarah looked forward to receiving her little table and the discussion it was sure to provoke.

Two Nights Only

I walked the streets of some terracotta-brick town in Mexico, killing time in the heat. This was my vacation from the other terracotta-brick town where I lived. My contract still had three months to run, so I thought I may as well see the country, but this place was mostly the same.

A truck behind me rumbled along in the traffic crawl with its loudspeaker message blaring. '*The circus is coming, for two nights only*.' I removed my headphones to listen better. There would be clowns, acrobats, children's characters — the usual. When the truck drew up, its thick bars cast a stripy shadow on the street and the flatbed metal roof flashed a sun-twinkled smile. Inside the makeshift cage was a tiger: a fully-grown actual tiger. I stopped walking and stared.

The animal was spread on the floor like pancake batter, head on its paws, displaying all of its size but none of its power or menace. Not a great advert for the circus. Perhaps it was car sick. It certainly wasn't pacing up and down, snarling through the bars as you might expect. The tiger looked out mournfully and I looked in — two foreigners locking eyes. Was this what I came to see, a dying version of the bad-old no-rules Mexico? Some people still pined for the days where scarred animals were corralled by moustached men in red coats and top hats.

The traffic lurched forward and the truck disappeared around the next corner. Before I knew what was happening, I was running. I desperately needed another look. As I rounded the corner onto the next street, the truck rested at the end of the block, waiting at a junction in the hundred-degree sun. The truck crossed the junction and continued. I wasn't sure if I would ever see it again.

As I ran, fruit stands and telephone poles positioned in the middle of the sidewalk did their best to stop me. The tiger remained tantalisingly out of reach, around forty yards ahead. I chased the thing for eight blocks, tracking its distance by its loudspeaker advertisement. My arm clamped my messenger bag to stop it from bouncing around as I ran. The traffic slowed, and I finally gained ground. The car in front was held at a red light.

When I came alongside, my chest heaved gulps of hot air and sweat poured from every part of me. My t-shirt clung to my back like a baby to its mother. Reaching into my bag, I dug out my camera before the lights could change. Head up. Stare into the soul of the beast. The tiger didn't move, it just stared at me with empty eyes like it was in a holding pattern, tired of waiting for home. Its stripes would bleach and fade in the picture. What good was it being so powerful if all you saw through the bars of your cage was another trapped animal?

I fanned myself with my cap, unsure if I was even going to take the picture. Then, the lights changed and the truck moved off, kicking up dust.

The hands that gripped the bulky camera lowered. Shallow breaths returned to normal. The sun blazed orange.

'*The circus is coming, for two nights only.*' The sound of the advertisement faded to quiet, then the truck turned right, and it was gone.

Falling Down

To Crystal Cornish
Her Majesty's Prison Peterborough
20th June

Dear Crystal Cornish,

I'm the reason you are in prison. Sorry about that. Please don't stop reading. Don't write me off as someone who plays tricks on convicted murderers. I know you're not guilty because I know who caused your boyfriend's death.

According to my therapist, guilt is harder to process than anger. That's probably why I'm such a wreck. But, you're the one suffering in prison. I really am sorry about that. Are you getting pushed around in there? You looked like a tough person when I saw you in the courtroom during the trial.

I'm not tough. I even got a bull terrier to make me feel safer. Peterborough is not the nicest place after dark. Stabbings and all that. The thing is, I can't stop thinking about what happened on the car park roof. I can't just sharpen the end of a toothbrush and stab guilt in the leg. By the way, does that actually happen in prison?

There's no way a guy like me could survive in prison. I'm an administrative assistant who plays World of Warcraft online. Yesterday, when a man with a shaved head asked me for directions, I crossed the street, thinking he was a skinhead football fan. Then, he told me he was a travelling monk and asked me if I wanted to know more about Buddhism. That's when I really panicked. The stupid thing was, I *did* want to know more about Buddism, but I'm so uptight at the moment, it's hard to say yes to anything. Sorry for going on, but it helps to write, and there's no one else I can talk to about this (apart from my therapist). You must feel the same, like everyone is out to get one over on you? Well, I'm not. Honestly. Will you give me the chance to explain myself?

Of course, I can't write what happened that day in a letter. I'm afraid that I'll end up where you are (well, not the women's prison, but jail). Does that make me a coward? The ladies in my office think I'm a pushover. They still treat me like a tea boy despite my promotion to Senior Administrator for Peterborough Council. They even have a running joke that I should transfer to Nottingham Council because of my name.

How do you fight back against bullies in prison? You must have your fair share. Unfortunately, violence is frowned upon in government offices.

Anyway, I've added some money to your commissary fund and included a picture of myself holding this letter. That way you'll know I'm not some bent copper trying to catfish you. I hope you can write back and I'll tell you more about what I know.

Daniel Nottingham.

To Daniel Nottingham
17B Weekley Road, Peterborough, Cambridgeshire.
25th June

Dear Sheriff of Nottingham (or whoever the fuck you are),

Is this some kind of joke? You think I'd trust you just cos you put a tenner in my prison account? I checked my back and there ain't no handle growing out of it, so I'm not a mug.

You look like that bloke in the boner pills advert — a bit skinny, but quite fit. You wouldn't last a week in prison, men's or women's. Maybe you should get your lookalike to sign up with the Buddhists and tell you what they are all about. Have you ever seen him? That bloke from the erectile dysfunction ads. I'd be laughing at the thought of you visiting if I wasn't locked up in here with nothing to do.

Dunno what you're going on about, really. Are you saying it was you who was responsible? I told the police a thousand times. Erol fell. I didn't push him. No one did. Don't bother telling your lies to my solicitor. That slimy prick never believed me, so I'm getting a new one for my appeal. It doesn't make sense, me wanting to kill Erol. He wasn't a gang member or nothing even though he did like to slap me about a bit. I was going to dump him anyway because he just got sacked from the phone shop. He was even more broke than me. If you know so much about what happened, prove it. Tell me your version of events — and don't leave out no details about Erol, the car park, and the time.

You probably didn't even see what he looked like. His head came apart like a Cadbury's cream egg. I only recognised his bomber jacket. I told that to *my* therapist. They call them 'councillors' in here, and they make you go.

Who cares if this is real? I'll answer your questions. Is everyone out to get me? Well, yeah. I'm a mixed-race girl from East London who has no job and an abusive, but dead boyfriend. Not many people see things the way I do. You get me?

You keep paying into my commissary and I'll help you deal with those bitches in your office. One — grow a beard. Literally, grow one. You look like a teenager. Too well-groomed. You wouldn't mess with the blokes on that Vikings show, so grow one like that. Glue one on if you have to. Or you can tell them that sheriffs get to carry a gun.

Remember, write me back with details or this is the last letter I'll write.

Crystal Cornish

27th June

Dear Crystal,

I wish I could grow a beard. The hair that grows is like hamster fur and without shaving, I resemble a fifteen-year-old trying to buy alcohol in a newsagent.

Honest to God, I promise you I'm not a Nigerian prince scammer or a member of the Cambridgeshire Constabulary. Also, I believe a prison psychologist is called a counselor. A 'Councillor' works for the local government, like me. I should know. Who would make up Senior Administrator for Peterborough Council as their job? I have the exit ticket from the car park. 1:58pm. That's exactly when it happened. Shall I bring the ticket when I visit? He was wearing a green bomber jacket. That's all I know because I only saw a crowd of people around him on the ground. That was the problem. I heard someone up there, but I didn't see him.

Please let me visit. I'll keep applying to the prison until you accept the request. You have to listen to my version. The therapist told me to stop coming today. I know it's been a few months since the incident, but I think the guilt is eating her more than it is me. Once she figured out I wasn't deluded she said I shouldn't incriminate myself and we should stop sessions. I didn't do anything illegal that day (apart from being five minutes late back to work).

The police wouldn't listen, nor my therapist. I don't have a girlfriend or a wife. Even my dog, Bilbo, won't listen, he's deaf in one ear. And before you ask about my family, I can't tell them either. It would break my mother's heart, learning that her son is responsible for such a tragedy. She won't even admit her son looks like the 'degenerate in that awful penile health advert'.

You have to hear me out. We can help each other. All you have to do is keep reading. So, the same day I was dumped by my therapist, I was forcibly removed from Peterborough Magistrates' Court. They banned me from requesting case notes because I'm not a lawyer. Does my new job title at the Council count for nothing? They've even processed a restraining order against me. Are you flattered that I care that much? Never thought I'd get a restraining order slapped on me by a building. You'll have to tell me what's going on with the appeal in your next letter.

Anyway, on the way back to the office, two teenagers gave me the crooked index finger, you know the sign the guy does on the advert. And then I read your letter not believing me about being a real person? If I had any more nonsense I might have gone full 'Falling Down' — you know that film about an office worker who goes on the rampage? Sorry, I didn't mean to mention falling again, but here we are.

Sandra (the office manager) ticked me off in front of my boss for clocking in three minutes late. I told her I came in twenty minutes before her this morning, and she was so miffed that she threatened to make it an HR issue. That night I was too jumpy to go out. What more could go wrong? Now I stay in. The pizza place has my order round in minutes. My dog's very happy with the pepperoni, but we're both putting on weight. So, that's my life. How's your day going?

I've added some more money to your commissary fund. What did you spend the last lot on?

Yours, Daniel.

P.S. Trust me, I'm not going anywhere.

2nd July

Dear Michael Douglas,

Don't get your willy in a twist. Thought you was a chicken who couldn't survive in prison, now you're chatting about going on the rampage? Fair enough, I believe you were there. Who else would be sad enough to make a visitors request every week? My mum has only come to see me once. Imagine that, your own mum thinking you're guilty. She loved Erol.

Sorry I didn't write back till now. They put me in solitary for fighting. That was your fault and all. Girls tried to take the stuff I bought with the money you sent, so I used your idea about the toothbrush.

It felt like three weeks in solitary. No exercise or TV or nothing. I dunno what they expect you to do — think, I suppose. I thought about how my cellmate, Natasha Greaves, and her mate, Curly, kept helping themselves to my stuff. It was only a little bit at first, chocolate bars or skin wipes. A few days ago I find out she's been paying off her debts with my pack of tampons, handing them out like cigarettes. Daft cow probably tried to smoke them too. They gave me three days in lock up and Natasha has a week in hospital.

So, here is my day so far. The C.O.s took me to my new cell. They were alright about it, bagged up my stuff, even the tampons. My new cellmate is a little pussy-mouse called Chloe. She won't tell me what she did, but I don't care. She speaks so low I can barely hear it. Makes a change from Tash with her foghorn Scottish accent. We did exercise at eleven. It was good to be outside. You don't know how you miss it until you are surrounded by these slimy walls. 12:30 was lunch — rubber chicken and mashed potatoes. I didn't kill Erol, but I could murder a KFC. In the afternoon I went to my English class. We get paid less than if we work, but you just have to read. I used to like books at school. English Lit was one of the only ones I passed. One of the other girls said she already spoke English, so she shouldn't have to come. The teacher said 'that's debatable.' Mugged her right off. I don't think the stupid mare knew what debateable meant. Evenings are the worst. After six it goes quiet. No TV, no pub, not even chat. Got nothing better to do than write to you.

Still no word about an appeal. It's getting boring now. They were in such a rush to lock me up, but now... I used to rage to the C.O.s about the broken sink in my cell, or about Tash and Curly. Don't even have them now. Just little mouse Chloe quivering on the bottom bunk.

If what you say is true, then I'm not angry at you, Daniel. I need to know what happened to Erol, about that day he jumped. Maybe none of this was your fault, but you have to tell the truth. No lies. I'm beginning to wonder if you even have erectile dysfunction.

See you next week.

Crystal.

10th July

Dear Crys, (can I call you that? It's just that Crystal makes me think of meth. I've been watching a lot of Breaking Bad and we all know what happened to *that* guy.)

Seeing as you appreciate my sense of humour, I'm tempted to make a 'time of the month' joke about your hell in a cell fight with Tash. Then again, I certainly don't want to get on your bad side. Keep sticking it to 'em anyway.

Thanks for letting me visit. I feel so much better after getting my side of the story across. I'll try and fill in the gaps of the story in this letter. After just thirty minutes, I feel I know you so much better than from your letters. You're quite sweet in person.

I wish I'd known what to expect from a prison. Nobody told me I'd feel so nervous. All those metal detectors and forms — it might be harder getting in than breaking out. It's lucky they allow books because I don't think the *Count of Monte Cristo* would have fit up my arse. I remembered you studied it. Have you started reading it yet?

I didn't tell you during the visit, but I nearly didn't come. Thought you might still be angry. Well, you were a *bit* angry. It was rotten of your family to cancel their visit without telling you.

Thanks for telling me I'm more handsome than the erectile dysfunction guy. You are not so bad yourself — even prettier than the older lady with the stomach problems in the Senokot ads. Anyway, I can assure you, everything is in order down there. From what you told me, there's more sex going on in your prison than in my one-bed flat. Mind you, it's been a while since my girlfriend ran off with her girlfriend. Honestly. She'd probably fit right in in E-block.

I said I'd answer your questions about my version of events, so here goes:

- That car park has no CCTV or number plate recognition because the Council won't pay for them to be installed.
- The owner of Toasties Cafe identified the guy who looks like me (possibly Mr. Floppy Cock) from the camera footage outside his shop. That's when they threatened to arrest me if I didn't stop wasting police time.
- I was watching the news because I don't have friends (well, non World of Warcraft friends) and there was nothing else on the telly. I saw the report about Erol falling from the top of the multi-storey. Recognised his green jacket, and one of the witnesses I saw on the way out. The reporter said they were holding you under suspicion of murder.

- I did hear a bump, but when I looked out of the rear-view, there was nothing there. Sometimes you imagine things, so I just drove off.

When the report finished, I picked up the phone and went to dial the police station. But how could I be sure? How could they check? Was it a good idea to show up after drinking two glasses of red wine like some tipsy reverend. I needed more time to think.

The next day, I sat in an uncomfortable plastic chair for two hours while they checked my story. I told them I wouldn't be seen dead in that sandwich shop because they put gherkins in their tuna melts *and* short-change people. The detective told me to leave. He must have thought I was your 'bit on the side' wanting to take the blame. I drove home in the same car that… you know.

Whom could I tell? Mother? My workmates? The World of Warcraft community? It would all just get more complicated. So I told my therapist and even she washed her hands of me.

You're an inspiration, Crys. The visit was great. Enjoy the book. You *will* get out, and when you do, we'll visit the town library, or maybe go to the cinema. I don't suppose you like online role-playing games.

Dan. (a.k.a Walter White).

13th July

World of Warcraft, Daniel? You better not be into any nasty dungeon master shit, or I'll stop writing.

This whole situation is so ridiculous. The police, the courts, nobody wants you to make the case more complicated. Except me. You have to share what you know with my new solicitor. He won't tell no one. Client-attorney privilege, that's what he tells me.

You can't keep it bottled up. I've seen girls go mental in here because of what's locked up in their heads. Maddy 'nine-fingers' nearly lost another one by kicking off in the dining hall. She's wrong in the head. The C.O. smacked her legs up with the stick, but she got it on the hand trying to protect herself. Maddy told them that she was going to sue, which gave us a laugh. If my conviction gets overturned, I won't see a penny. Know that.

I thought about you a lot after your visit. I'd go to the library with you. Course. There's no free WiFi here and my cellmate is always asking me questions I don't know the answers to.

I'm not going to tell you about the appeal date. If you show up at the courthouse, you'll get done for violating your restraining order, and that will delay the trial. I can't be doing with another three months in here. I trust my new solicitor, Mr Moncrief. At least he's got a posh name. He seems confident 'we' can beat this. I told him 'we' don't have to look through our porridge for roaches or wonder where the carrots and cucumbers have been before they get put on our plates. 'We' don't have to keep a shiv gripped in our hands during yard time in case Curly or Tash try want payback.

Moncrief says he got hold of footage from a ticket machine showing me coming past with a cig, two minutes after Erol's big splat. The witness who said he saw us together on the top of the car park is going on the stand again. If he admits he was wrong, I could be out of here.

You best print me a library card ready for my release. I hope you are senior enough for that, Mr Administrator.

Crys.

To Crystal Cornish
Flat 8B Cambridge Heights, South Bretton, Peterborough, Cambridgeshire
3rd August,

Dear Countess of Monte Cristo,

Congratulations on getting out. I knew they couldn't keep you locked up in a maximum-security after the case fell apart. What a turn of events at the hearing! Did you recognise me in my Hasidic Jew costume? Sorry I didn't follow instructions, but I had to see you, to know what would happen. I would have loved to see the faces of the crown prosecutors, but you know… I got forcibly removed.

This is the first time they've allowed me to write a letter. It's been two days since your release and my incarceration. Most of the guards think it's stupid writing a letter. I only got seven days for breach of the restraining order, so I might reach you before the post does. Still, I didn't actually think they would follow through on the threat to imprison me for attending a trial. The bloke in the costume shop said no one would recognise me with the wig and the beard, and the hat and robes. I've probably lost the deposit on it too because it's in the personal effects lockup with the rest of my stuff.

I'm glad I'm not in a maximum security like you were. I was terrified when they transported me straight from the courtroom to the lockup. That's what they call it: lockup. The guards couldn't stop laughing about the costume. It wasn't so funny for me.

It's not as dangerous as HMP Peterborough. In fact, I'm probably safer here than out in Peterborough city centre on a Friday night. My cellmate is a secretary. One of the other men is an HR representative serving time for filing false sexual harassment claims. We're all administrators. I may as well start my own gang because I've lost my job by now. I'm a criminal. No self-respecting council in all of England will employ me. Not even Nottingham.

They don't assign short-term prisoners a counselor. So, I went to church and saw the chaplain. The man was very pushy, asked me a hell of a lot of questions about my beliefs. I thought it best not to tell him about the disguise I wore to get into the court, or my subsequent removal. I didn't tell Mother why I can't answer my phone, or why she has to feed Bilbo for the week. I told the chaplain my sentence was for violating a restraining order, so at least I haven't lied in the eyes of God. Do you think Erol will forgive me?

It takes a week to get clearance to request library books, so I've got nothing to read, apart from a copy of the Bible the chaplain lent me. Maybe that's how they get you. Have you read anything since you got out? I bet your mother was glad to see you. Have you forgiven her for thinking you were guilty? I could always come over in my Rabbi outfit to convince her of the real story. People respect Rabbis.

I can't wait to see you, Crystal. I can't wait to hug you, to make plans about what awful jobs us ex-cons might manage to get. You can meet Bilbo, we can eat pizza together, and maybe take a road trip to Nottingham.

What do you say?

Inmate 1596A

9th August,

Dear Inmate 1596A,

This letter should be waiting for you when you get home. I'll be around this afternoon to meet Bilbo and welcome you.

Life has been alright since getting out. It's been nearly a week now. Mostly I'm getting used to having a phone again and eating what I want. My mum is so jumpy around me now I've been inside. It's like she's not sure what I might do. You might be the only person who understands the experience (even though *your* prison sounds peak).

I owe you one for the info you gave Moncrief. He proved the witness who saw Erol fall would have seen me on top of the car park, too. Only I wasn't there. Can't wait to tell you more about the trail this afternoon when the pizza arrives. I'll get a bottle of red wine too, even though I prefer rum and coke. We could even stay in and watch that Michael Douglas film. What do you reckon?

Townies

Summer '97 was supposed to be one big party. Two weeks of sunset cocktails and trance euphoria in our dream destination. But after what Gavin Brunson did, I can never go back to Majorca.

I had finished my A-Levels and my relationship with an immature boyfriend, and was looking forward to soaking up the rays and watching my heroes work their magic on the decks. Magaluf a.k.a. 'Shagaluf' was the number one clubbing destination back then. The best of the best played the Carwash and Club Coco Bongos — Oakenfold, Judge Jules, Sasha & Digweed. Gavin was a DJ too, or so he claimed. Last I heard, he was doing car park raves, still clinging onto dreams of superstardom in his forties. Now that he's gone to prison for a long time, there's no point in keeping his secret any longer. Sometimes the search for fame kills. I can prove it.

Mum dropped John-Boy and me at Stansted Airport. The others were already at check-in.

'Hi Lauren. Hi Kels.' We had a little group hug.

'Alright Katie, babes,' said Kelly. 'That lanky git got leave I see.'

John-Boy pretended not to hear, but I knew he still had feelings for her. He went off to look in Dixons with Gavin. Back then, Gavin was just a loud-mouthed telesales rep with West Ham tattoos and too much hair gel.

There were six of us in total. Lauren, who worked at Mum's salon, was a couple of years older than me. Her friend Kelly was my brother's ex. Gavin had taken on the role of finding another person to take Mark's place after we broke up. I thought he'd bring along another 'diamond geezer', but his mate looked young and geeky.

'Oh, hello there. I'm Nathan,' he said, raising up on his toes like he was trying to look over a wall. No spikey hair and gold chains; his polo shirt was buttoned all the way up to the top, even though it was hot. His shorts were too short and his hair was too long. I returned his wave, and Gavin whacked his arm.

'What did I tell you, Nate. Bit skinny but John-Boy's little sis is alright, eh?'

I'd never seen a black guy go red before.

He turned to Gavin, annoyed. 'I told you, it's Nathan, not Nate.'

'Alright, mate. Just chill.'

We survived the journey on the noisy charter flight and were first to get off the bus, as our 'brand new' accommodation was a little out of town. Concrete slabs and rebar littered the unturned gardens. Our new accommodation was a construction site. Still, the holiday complex had a small shop so we stocked up on wine and crisps and went back to unpack.

Gavin snatched a pair of Nathan's shorts and ran into the lounge with them. 'Ooh, nice swimmers, mate,' he said, parading around. 'You'll look like a black David 'assel'off in these.'

Nathan ignored him and carried on unpacking.

Gavin wouldn't leave it. 'Oi, Nathan. Are you even old enough to watch Baywatch?'

'Leave off him,' said Kelly. 'You'd probably play the cheesy theme song at Pacha on a Saturday night hoping to get some action.'

'And you probably think the Ministry of Sound is a governmental department,' John-Boy shot back. He laughed and Gavin swaggered over and high-fived him.

We started on the bottles of Lambrini, lemonade and cheap vodka and the party was on. Gavin, the designated tunesmaster, blasted the bass from his speakers. We shoved the lounge furniture to the wall to create a dance floor. Clothes scattered everywhere. That night we let loose. I suppose, people back home would have called us townies — young, loud and brash — but we didn't care. Magaluf was every towny's dream.

We took the long walk into town and joined the swarms attracted to the neon-lit bars like randy insects. A rep outside The Carwash beckoned us.

'What's up, guys? Having a good night, no?' His chest hair burst through his Hawaiian shirt. His name badge said 'Eros'.

Our responses varied from wild whoops, to Lauren dancing down the street in her own world.

'Hey. Any of you connected to any DJs?'

Gavin pushed his way to the front of the group. 'DJs? Yes mate, that's me.'

Eros lifted his shades. 'Cool. Cool. I've got this track, you know? Trying to get it into the clubs.'

'Sweet,' said Gavin, patting him on the shoulder. 'What sort of vibe?'

Eros lowered his voice. 'The sort that makes the ladies crazy. You'll see.'

Gavin looked impressed. He said he was mates with Gary Revs and could ask him to spin it.

'I no recommend to listen, my friend. You have to listen with the women. It's like the Viagra. I call it Afrodisiac. It gets a hold of people and they can never forget it.'

By that point, Gavin had half a gram of coke in him. He rabbited away with his new mate Eros while John-Boy and I chased after Lauren. When we came back Gavin had the CD gripped in his hand like a grenade. 'Eros says it's a never-fail.' He performed several clumsy winks at Kelly and me. 'I'll be banging all night long to this as soon as we get some proper birds back to the flat.'

***

The hangover smacked me about the next morning. Nathan and I were up first. A skinny girl slipped out of John-Boy's room, collected her bag and started her walk of shame. A muscular club rep bowled out of Kelly's room twenty minutes later. He pulled on a t-shirt that said Bobby Dazzler above a large number one.

'Morning all,' he said in a sunshine tone, then went over to the kitchen sink and splashed his face with water. 'Laters.' And with that, he strode out. He'd obviously done that before.

I looked over at Nathan. 'Unbelievable. I suppose for boys, it's a walk of pride.'

'Mmm,' he said between mouthfuls of cereal.

I asked how he slept.

'As well as expected. Think we were the only ones who didn't wake up next to strangers this morning,' he said. 'That music…'

They had been noisy. Spinning records in the lounge until six, then noises from the bedroom too. Packing earplugs was a stroke of genius on my part.

As I poured myself a cup of tea, Nathan lowered his voice. 'I think Lauren and Gavin… you know.'

'Never. Lauren would never—'

'They were in the room next to mine. Sounded like a pair of wounded animals.'

Lauren and Gavin? On the first night of our holiday? Apart from me, she was the sensible one. She saved money, kept her head down at the salon.

At one o'clock, Lauren finally emerged from Gavin's lair. She ran straight for the bathroom, crying and jabbering all sorts, not making any sense. I told we'd all done things we regretted.

Her hair and makeup was a mess when she came out. 'I wasn't even drunk. Last thing I remember was dancing in the lounge. Gavin put that guy's CD on.'

I looked at Nathan, trying not to laugh. *Afrodisiac*. According to Lauren, that music was 'Voodoo shit.'

John-Boy played it down. So did Gavin. The mixtape wasn't important, it just had the usual Radio 1 stuff. Like an unknown piece of home-recorded keyboard music could have magic powers.

Over the next week, Nathan and I spent afternoons talking at the beach. I even read the book he lent me. At night we hit the clubs, dancing to the season's hottest beats. Amazingly, Gavin kept up his hot streak. Almost every morning there would be a different girl, slinking out of our apartment, wondering what had happened. No one else was getting so much action and he wasn't exactly rich or charming.

In the flat, we talked about one thing — the contents of that CD. He carried it with him wherever he went. Even John-Boy never caught another glimpse of it. Gavin strutted around that week as if he owned Magaluf. A spikey haired red rooster. He even blagged a DJ slot at one of the smaller clubs.

Nathan said his connection to Gavin was kind of embarrassing.

I touched his arm. 'It can't be more embarrassing than Lauren and all those others...'

Nathan's mum was behind on payments for a TV he sold her. He was going to call the debt collectors and take the thing back. Apparently, Nathan's house got visits from bailiffs all his life. 'My mum's got a credit card problem.' He looked out across the sea, past the party boats and cruise ships. 'He said if I took this holiday package, I could pay him back in instalments before Christmas, and he would give my mum an extra three months on the TV deal too.'

'Wow. Well, you're having a good time aren't you?'

He flashed white teeth. 'Yeah. I'm happy I came. I'm pleased we met, Katie.'

On our way back from the beach, we went by The Carwash for a drink and I saw an opportunity to solve the mystery of the mixtape. I asked the Spanish barman when Eros would be working. 'Eros. Big sunglasses, tall guy. He works here.'

'No, no, my darling. Carwash have no one called Eros.' The barman shrugged and continued polishing the bar, preparing for another night of debauchery.

***

The next Saturday we got to Tall Trees early. Gavin was hoping that Gary Revs, the opening act DJ would let him spin his mixtape. He'd even gone so far as to get the CD pressed onto vinyl.

In Magaluf, nothing gets going early. Before midnight it's just sticky floors and old posters which are usually hidden by the hundreds of sweaty bodies. The beats echoed over the empty dance floor and us girls chipped in for a very expensive pitcher of sex on the beach. Most of the hundred-or-so crowd were sixteen-year-olds with fake IDs. Bouncers are less vigilant when a club is half full. Two hours remained until the headliners, Garnier and Fatboy Slim, played.

'After this shit goes down, we'll be VIP,' said Gavin, holding his record up for us to see. 'You'll see. It's unstoppable. I'll be immortal.'

Lauren said it wasn't possible to clear the dancefloor any more.

Gavin ignored her. He strode off towards Gary Rev in the DJ booth. 'G-Man's coming.' Just saying his DJ name now makes me shudder. He was already insufferable, but he'd be downright dangerous if he got famous.

After a few words, Gary Rev passed his headphones over to Gavin and signalled that he was off to smoke a cigarette. Gavin went to work mixing his record seamlessly with the funky house on the decks.

Lauren wanted us to stop him from playing the track. I told her to chill out.

Within one minute of Gavin fading in the music, the dance floor was covered. The beat ripped girls out of their seats, me included. The boys followed. Soon, the VIP booths were empty, and the bar was deserted. Laser lighting pulsed over the bodies on the dance floor. DJ G-man raised his arms like he was some kind of God.

The music was like nothing I'd heard before; it took control of my body. He was right, it was unstoppable. Bass pumped the sound system, fusing deep house rhythms and tribal drumming patterns.

Our organs pumped and our heads clouded. Sweeping synths and melodies intertwined and a sexy vocal line of 'oohs' and 'aahs' rose and fell to the beat. It was like eight tracks together, so natural, like a sort of life energy. Whoever made this music had captured the feeling of ecstasy without any need for taking a pill.

Revellers danced, grinding and touching each other. A switch had been flipped. Suddenly, Nathan and I were sharing a long passionate kiss. It felt right. Our inner fires mixed and burned hot. Others around us threw off items of clothing. We charged with a feeling that had to burst out. It was a primal attraction, bodies pressed together.

Lauren yanked my arm and pulled me out of the throng.

'This is amazing!' I said.

She shielded my ears from the music, leaned in and shouted. 'It only works once.'

'What?' I said, pulling away, desperate to get back to music, back to Nathan.

She held me firm and spoke into my ear. 'Fight it, Katie. This music drives girls crazy the first time they hear it, but after that, it's gone. It only works once.' She pointed to herself, the one person completely immune to the draw of the beat.

She had pulled out the plug. I clamped my hands to my ears and scanned the club. John-Boy was dancing, but not with the same intensity as the wide-eyed girls who were first-time listeners. Gavin was watching his handiwork from the DJ booth, dreaming of the havoc he could cause as the sole owner of the perfect club aphrodisiac.

Lauren squeezed my hand. 'We've got to stop this. Get everyone to snap out of this. Gavin can't—'

'All those one-night stands were because of this… this song?'

'Exactly.'

I don't know many men who could be trusted with a piece of music so special. Gavin salivated in the booth, an aggressive dog, licking his chops at the years of fresh meat. This record could set him up for life. The world didn't need that.

Gary Revs had returned from his smoke break and stared, mouth agape at the dancers. What the hell was going on? I took advantage of the distraction, reached over the booth and ripped the record off the turntable. It caught the needle and let out a screech over the speakers. Gavin whipped around, his face a violent red. Confused dancers, drew out of their trance.

'Oi, what the fuck are you doing, Katie?'

What did I expect? I just wanted anyone to have that record but him. I tossed the vinyl to Lauren and she hurried towards the exit.

Murmurs and shouts grew on the dance floor. The ecstasy of a few moments before, dissipated. 'Hey, what is this?' 'What the—?' The spell of Eros broke and we stood in an underwhelming, half-empty club again.

Gavin jumped down onto the dance floor and raised his fist. 'If you weren't John-Boy's sister I'd knock your fucking teeth down your throat.' He ground his own teeth together. Nathan put himself between us, stepping an inch away from Gavin's face.

'Oi, Lauren,' he said, looking past Nathan. She turned.

Nathan held him back, but Gavin reared back and brought his head full force into Nathan's face. *Crack.* Nathan crumpled, clutching at his broken nose. Gavin shoved his way through the crowd. A bearded doorman in a bomber jacket was over quickly. Gavin swung for him and missed. The sea of dancers parted, creating enough room for the bouncer to hold him down.

'You can't take it, you bitch,' he shouted. 'It's going to make me famous.'

Without looking back, I raced to catch up with Lauren. I knew what I had to do. There was no time to check on Nathan. I hailed a taxi and went straight back to the apartment. John-Boy would have to deal with Gavin.

When I got back to the flat I took a fire extinguisher to Gavin's door and searched his room. The CD wasn't in the stereo, but after going through his drawers, I found it under his grimy underwear. He had written the names of the six girls he had slept with inside the case. Disgusting. I tried to snap the disc. No dice. It was too strong — reinforced with metal or something. The kitchen knife I grabbed made no mark on the metal side. It was bulletproof, don't ask me how. If I chucked it in the freezer, I could break it in two later. No one else would ever hear Afrodesiac's beats again. As I waited for the others, I

123

listened to the gentle crash of waves from the beach and the sounds of Magaluf in the distance.

When Lauren, Nathan and Kelly came back two hours later we agreed that Gavin Brunson wasn't welcome anymore. Nathan held an ice pack to his nose. He'd live. John-Boy was still talking to the police.

***

What more is there to say about that summer? The police gave Gavin a couple of hours in a cell and a slap on the wrist, even though he attacked two people and nearly reconfigured the laws of human attraction.

Twenty years on, the group are all in different places. Lauren bought into the salon and runs it with Mum, who works part-time now. John-Boy stayed in the army and did tours of Afghanistan and Iraq. He works from a desk nowadays, which suits his wife. Kelly moved to Birmingham and keeps in touch with Lauren. And Nathan? Well, we're still together, twenty years and counting, married for twelve. We still love dance music, that'll never change. Our kids laugh at our sad old music.

John-Boy kept us updated on Gavin's life. He stayed in Majorca for the season, looking for Eros, asking half the islanders where he could get a copy of Afrodesiac. He searched online, asked in record shops, wrote to music magazines. After he struck out, he returned to wheeling and dealing in London to finance his search for the tune. He convinced himself that one song could make him a top club DJ. That nutter even hired private investigators. He paid experts to try and recreate the track.

Two weeks ago, the Rochester Times reported that Gavin Brunson had been found guilty of first-degree murder. I don't get any satisfaction out of a 'told you so', but people like him are bad to the core. Perhaps this story explains why a man would bludgeon his wife to death with a Technics PLX turntable for messing with the settings on his MIDI keyboard.

Magaluf has gone downhill. They've banned drinking on the street and most of the big dance music acts play Ibiza or unpronounceable festivals in The Balkans or Dubai. Nathan is the one good thing that came out of that trip. We've been happy, in Essex, living our towny lives. That track brought us together. I've never told him that I hid the CD in the freezer, or that I took it back with me for safe keeping. In fact, I've never been able to part with it. Maybe one day I'll give it another spin.

Cherry Orchards

Piotr tapped his signet ring on the metal seat in front of him. He watched the 'distance to destination' clock tick down one tenth of a mile at a time. After months of planning, he couldn't afford to attract suspicion by arriving late to his simulation appointment, but the driverless bus inched along, stuck in the block grey outskirts of Sheffield.

A girl with tattooed hands unscrewed the top to her lip balm and released its synthetic cherry smell. Piotr still remembered the sharp taste of the fruit from when he lived in Poland — before the fallout from the power facilities and the mass-migration that followed. Back when he was a boy, his mother would send him out to find the fruiting trees in the abandoned groves. Piotr filled the buckets she gave him and ate as many as he could stomach. His family had stayed behind with the dying trees.

The synchronised bleep from passengers' smartwatches told him oh-nine hundred had arrived and the bus came to a stop outside the Department of Wellbeing, Cognitive Section. If he hurried, he might make it into the building before nine-o-one. Piotr pushed his way in front of the groups of workers and walked towards the entrance double-quick. He scanned his lifecode at the entry barrier and received clearance to enter. The double-height glass doors opened. *Only one minute late.* Government employees filtered through access-code barriers and Piotr was left unaccompanied, standing in the mirrored lobby. The operators of The Simulator would be watching him, observing that day's subject. He waited for instructions.

Although he was about to steal information which could result in an espionage conviction, Piotr waited with no nervous pacing around the hard floor or inspection of his receding hairline in the mirror. He thought about his colleague from Metropolitan Hospital, Dorota. She wouldn't be able to resist checking for grey hairs or crows-feet wrinkles, even though she looked younger than her forty-six years. The jokes they shared in the break room made the dull days pass quicker in ways AI interactions couldn't replicate. What would she think about Piotr's heist? As the minutes passed, he found himself revisiting summers spent in the countryside, before his parents were quarantined in the Warsaw fallout district and he left for England. Collateral damage. The images of green hillsides calmed Piotr and stopped him sweating under the glare of the lights.

Piotr resisted the urge to fidget with his hands and did his best to look bored of waiting. The Simulator was designed to make citizens more productive — to show them the best versions of themselves. Most test subjects sought the answer as to what their ambition was. Piotr already knew. He had already achieved his ambition of becoming a brain surgeon, but found the reality of performing 'cognitive realignment' procedures unsatisfying. Now, he wanted to go deeper, and help develop organic intelligence by building his own machine.

Without warning, the doors slid open, revealing a corridor with a deep red carpet and smooth walls. As he passed into the space, he saw a single painting of sunflowers in a vase placed above a computer terminal. Real flowers would have been too much trouble to change. No pictures celebrated the history of The Simulator, and no photographs gave clues of the previous citizens randomly selected for trials. The computer displayed a consent form stating that he'd read the pre-testing materials and agreed to the terms of the trial. Piotr touched his index finger to the signature reader. Following the instructions, he removed his smartwatch and his grandfather's signet ring and placed them in the box provided. The doors slid shut behind him.

A woman in a navy suit entered through a panel which showed no signs of being a door. Piotr felt a little underdressed in his tracksuit, but he wanted to appear at ease. The woman's lapel badge indicated she was the subject liaison officer. Her face was as plain and expressionless as the walls of the building. 'Good morning,' she said. 'This way, Mr Woyzeck.'

They walked down long corridors, through heavy doors guarded by armed men. These machines carried more value than the lives of the hundreds of test subjects that used them each year. Piotr understood enough about memory to know the procedure could endanger something critical, like the already grainy mental images of his departed family. As they walked, the suited women reminded Piotr of the need to create an 'earth', a strong image that would help guide him out of simulated vision and back to reality. For the second time that day, he pictured cherry trees.

'The team will perform the procedure here.' She motioned through a glass panel to the examination room.

A brown leather recliner drew his eyes to the centre of the tiled floor. Control boards studded the sides of the room, two-way mirrors above them. Two technicians in blue uniforms and face masks punched in commands.

Piotr was familiar with the process — first the headpiece, then the epidural tap. He listened to the safety briefing with his hands in his tracksuit pockets. Then, he extracted the tiny transfer chip from its casing and pinched it between his finger and thumb. One quick movement was all it would take. The projected vision of his future would begin slowly and increase in pace. Real-time physical readings would cross-reference with his life data and the questionnaire he'd completed. The code he planned to extract would enable Piotr to run his own simulations through the machine in his room in the city centre.

The technician approached with the aluminium headpiece. Piotr did his best to avoid his heartbeat climbing to a suspicious rate. Just before the man tightened the metal band, Piotr held up his hand.

'Just a second.'

The technician glared.

He inserted his index finger under the contact pad and pressed the transfer chip onto the skin on his right temple. He scratched up and down at his imaginary itch. 'That's better.'

The technicians looked at each other for a moment. Had they seen the chip? The taller one lowered his mask as if he was going to say something. He scratched at his neck under his beard and replaced the mask. The men continued their work.

Piotr closed his eyes. The key to forecasting human potential came from stimulating positive memories, like those Piotr had of pre-disaster Poland. Yet, the stronger the amplification, the greater the likelihood of those memories getting warped or destroyed. Apart from his grandfather's ring, he didn't have a single possession to remind him of that time. The Simulator was a delicate balance of progress and ruin — it could push people towards their perfect form or leave them as empty shells. Even if it meant breaking the law, Piotr would find the advantage human brains had over the AI-run empires.

'Relax your body, sir,' said the technician, with the same indifference that Piotr showed during his surgery observations. 'The machine will find its— ah, we're in.'

Piotr hadn't felt the needle enter his back even though he'd seen the size of it in the instructional video. In fact, he'd watched all the videos that existed, read the books written by the machine's creators and even belonged to an online community which shared information about trying to reverse engineer the technology for the benefit of all. That was something he'd left out on his pre-trial questionnaire.

He thought he'd be excited, eager to get a look at the equipment and experience his first real 'vision', but now he was here, a tranquillity washed over him, like he didn't need to worry about petty things such as his impending life-partnership match or his career. The sensation, he imagined, was what opioid medication felt like — floating on high.

A voice, which seemed distant, asked if Piotr was ready.

He gave the signal. 'Begin.'

A jolt of current went through the metal headpiece and the transfer of memories and data commenced. As the moving pictures of his life events ran through the next few days, then months, Piotr lived his potentialised life at an ever-increasing speed. He saw himself working on his own simulator, making a breakthrough and actualising a live test. His future self seemed stable, important, happy. He was back at the Department of Wellbeing but it seemed brighter and more welcoming. The staff knew him. He had a passcode. The pace of the simulation quickened. People, events and thoughts blurred into each other, but in his drug-induced haze, Piotr understood them all as if he'd lived them.

The distant voice returned. 'Visuals are off the charts... over-exposure... should we keep running?'

Piotr did not panic. He was not fully cognisant of the danger, and he accepted it. He needed as much data on his transfer chip as possible, even if it meant he lost part of his brain function permanently. The visualisations had jumped forward several lifetimes, and in the partial images that followed he got a fleeting glance of worlds beyond his comprehension as a neurologist. People had harnessed technology to grow their brain function, not just to mimic it.

'Grounding subject.'

The visions in Piotr's mind dissolved into the image of a fruit orchard. He felt the breeze on his skin and the dappled sun shining through the branches of the trees. The blues, greens and reds of his childhood returned. Instead of viewing his life through a lens, Piotr felt himself sitting in the leather recliner once again. He opened his eyes to white light.

The technicians had removed their masks and were talking in hushed voices in the corner of the room. Piotr thought he heard them mention a 'development program' with more tests. When they noticed he was conscious, they stopped talking and returned to the middle of the room. One of the technicians disconnected the headpiece while the other powered down the machine. Piotr sat upright with a jolt. The chip.

He made a grab for the headpiece, still in the technician's hands. 'Can I take one last look?'

The man eyed him suspiciously. He handed it over. 'Careful.'

Piotr studied the connections and display lights with great intensity while he felt for the chip with his right hand. 'Amazing technology,' he said, turning it over. Finally, he detected the chip bedded into the pad. He scratched it with a finger. 'I can't wait to find out my results.'

The technician reached for the device and began to pull it from Piotr's grasp. Just before he lost grip of it, Piotr managed to work the chip free and extract it under a fingernail.

The second technician spoke. 'Place your hand on the table, Mr Woyzeck, palm up,' he ordered.

Piotr stiffened. If his pulse were still being measured, it would have shown over one hundred and forty beats per minute. He slowly placed his hand on the table.

The man looked up to meet Piotr's eyes. 'I didn't realise you were left-handed.'

Piotr managed to stutter something about being ambidextrous. In his right hand, still hidden under the recliner, he squeezed the chip further under his nail.

'Very well. I'll attach these sensors to conduct your exit tests.'

As Piotr nodded a bead of sweat ran down the armpit of his outstretched arm. The technicians attached the clips to his hand and gave him the full repertoire of reaction tests, then took some blood. He managed to work the chip out from his fingernail and into the protective case in his trousers. Then, with the two technicians either side of him, Piotr marched down the sparse corridors in silence.

The subject liaison officer greeted him with his results. This was the moment where subjects discovered what they could become, and what they might achieve in life. She looked at the results screen in front of her and sighed. 'Well...'

'Is anything the matter?' asked Piotr, trying to act like the results were more important than the chip currently housed on the inside of his waistband. He leaned forward.

'I'm sorry, sir. It says here, you're to report tomorrow at o-nine hundred to discuss your results.' She didn't exactly look encouraging.

'All right then,' said Piotr, 'shame you can't tell me anything right now.' Once he got back to his apartment he'd have twenty hours to modify his own simulator design and upload the data. Twenty-one hours before they came looking for him. He turned to go.

'Wait,' said the woman sharply.

He held his breath and turned around.

'You forgot these,' she said, holding up his watch and signet ring.

Piotr rode the lift up to the twentieth floor of his accommodation tower. He resisted the temptation to check the transfer chip for damage. The carpeted corridors were almost as bare as those in the Department of Wellbeing and a lot older. Patches of wear showed the path of the residents' soles going to and from the lift, but it was rare for Piotr to encounter any of his neighbours. When he pressed his fingerprint to the panel of unit 20-139, the door to his room slid open.

He shuffled in through the narrow hallway and sat on the wooden stool in the alcove which connected his bed space and shower cubicle. Piotr extracted the chip from his waistband and inspected it for scratches. Nothing. Above him, screwed to the shelving racks, were rows of processors, illuminated by flashing red lights and cooled by the whirr of built-in fans. He looked at his watch. Twenty hours to conduct his experiment.

Before Piotr connected his metal headpiece and pinched it tight around the temple, he thought about his parents dying their slow death in Warsaw. That familiar lump returned to his throat. He was their compensation, gifted a new life and a good education in Britain. In his mind's eye, they waved at him from their modest house. Would they be proud of their son, a criminal? He inserted the data chip into the control panel positioned in his lap and modified the parameters of the simulation to match those from the official test. For the Government, the machine was simply a tool to improve their geopolitical standing, but for Piotr, The Simulator was an obsession; it was the bridge between now and forever, the solution to automated lifestyles programmed to put commercial interests ahead of human suffering.

Piotr felt for the entry point of the previous epidural tap. The puncture mark was too small to detect by touch, but a stinging pain told him when he'd found the wound. Piotr jabbed the needle into place and depressed the plunger. He exhaled and braced himself. These were the last of the drugs that Dorota had rescued from the hospital incineration unit.

The concoction of out-of-date painkillers and lucent serums hit his bloodstream like a bus crashing through a wall. He slumped onto the alcove partition behind him and the syringe dropped to the floor.

This time the images arrived at a much faster pace than his previous efforts. Piotr saw himself go to work and watched the 3D printer fill holes in brain-surgery patients' skulls. He ate lunch with Dorota. When he returned to his room, he worked on his homemade simulator, tinkering with the apparatus and code. He viewed himself from above, conducting tests, but could not see the visualisations his simulated avatar experienced. Did this version of himself know even more? Going one level deeper was surely the key to exponential human potential. The pace of his life events quickened, but he never made the major breakthrough he hoped for. Piotr lived a long life, fathered children, and ended his career as a respected surgeon.

He needed to picture his 'earth' image, but rather than grounding himself and exiting the simulation after one cycle, Piotr allowed the system to recalibrate and start again. It might be his last chance to find the key that unlocked the human mind. Anyway, by the time he was due back for his return appointment, they would have discovered the data breach. He had to continue.

Piotr's brain moved forward and generated the next simulation at an even faster pace. He sought to improve on his choices and their outcomes. His simulated life flashed by and took him further away from his earth image of a cherry orchard. This time, he successfully altered his machine. He put on a headset, one with more advanced looking controls. Piotr watched himself insert the epidural and set the test parameters. As he watched his avatar flip the data transfer switch, Piotr's mind cast him into the new vision. A deeper level of virtuality. What he saw amazed him. By realising ideas born in multiple-level simulations, people could shape the future however they chose. With this technology, the functions of the organic brains were limitless.

But, there was no time for Piotr to process his breakthrough. His torso, still slumped against the alcove wall, pulsed with the flow of information of his homemade machine. The system rebooted again and cast him straight into another simulation. Piotr's thought processes, his multiple-level projections and imagined lives became ever quicker and more powerful. He watched as humans realised their dream of spreading the species throughout the galaxy; they travelled back and forth in space and in time, they lived for centuries and they fixed the impossible problems of previous generations. There would be no more automated disasters like in Poland.

After one hour plugged into his updated simulation, Piotr had lived hundreds of lives, going deeper and deeper into the visual loop. He could no longer ground himself to exit. The most knowledgeable being that had ever lived was trapped within the confines of his own mind, sitting in a tiny Sheffield flat.

Searing pain shot through Piotr's back, up to the base of his skull and deep into his forehead. His eyes and mouth clamped shut in shock. He couldn't feel his legs.

'Piotr, you there?' The voice sounded close but he couldn't tell from which direction it came.

He managed to force his dry eyes open and light from the window and the open door flooded in. It was morning.

'Let's help you up.' The voice belonged to Dorota. She must have used her guest code to get into the apartment.

Piotr rubbed his temples and found some kind of metal clamped to his head. Surely, that was the source of the pain. A hand touched his cheek and a pair of green eyes stared into his. How long had he been sitting on the stool?

Even in his exhausted state, Piotr wanted to make notes from what he could remember of the incredible new worlds he'd visited. There was so much to record, but it was fading, just as dreams slip away in the moments after waking. Each iteration of the experience evaporated with every passing second. Piotr heard the sound of boots marching up the hallway, stopping outside unit 20-139. There was a pause. 'Get me some paper,' he said. 'I need to—'

Before Piotr could finish his thought, a team of men barged into the apartment, crowding the tiny space and blocking the exit. 'Step away, ma'am. We need to speak to Mr Woyzeck.' Dorota protested but they shoved her out into the corridor.

After a few seconds, Piotr's eyes adjusted to the light to see two security men in uniforms. They couldn't just gain access to his space. They didn't have the right.

'A missing person report was logged when you failed to attend your appointment,' said one of the men. 'Subject looks dangerously dehydrated,' he said to his colleague. 'Administering fluids.'

Piotr tried to turn his head, but his reactions were slow. The men held a sports bottle to his mouth, pinched his nose and squeezed. 'Hold still.' Through his splutters, they forced in the liquid. Piotr winced as they ripped out the epidural tap. He recognised the bearded man in front of him but wasn't sure from where. Piotr couldn't even remember connecting himself to the machine in the room with all of its blinking lights. The pain behind his eyes throbbed. Was he going to vomit?

'Sir, we are detaining you on suspicion of possessing classified information. We will continue this interview at the Department of Wellbeing. Do you understand?'

Piotr drifted in and out of consciousness, still thinking about committing what he'd experienced to paper.

The flat smelled odd, sterile somehow.

The second security man was fixing restraints to the woman in front of him. She struggled to regain the use of her arms. 'What did you see, Piotr?' she shouted. 'Tell me.'

Piotr held the bridge of his nose to alleviate the pain behind his eyes. 'Where we're going,' he said, 'and how to get there.'

The security men lifted him onto a portable gurney and began checking his vitals. One of them removed the headpiece and Piotr fell back into a deep sleep.

***

Piotr looked through the wide window into the examination room. The team was ready to conduct the first test. On the other side of the glass were ten subjects seated in their brown recliners and above them on the back wall, a painting of sunflowers in a vase. They had been selected to represent the nation: men and women of different ages, ethnicities, intelligence types. Although he'd never spoken to them, he felt like he knew them from the questionnaires they'd completed and their reactions to the preliminary tests.

He still suffered the pain behind his eyes most days, but today Piotr felt upbeat. He and the others running the program were doing the right thing. In the right hands, human-directed AI could improve lives.

'Test Subject One, ready?'

The teenager wore an anxious expression. She crossed her arms, revealing the black and green tattoos on her hands.

Piotr called the other test subjects in turn over the intercom. He watched as they responded and looked to each other for support. After months of work, he was ready to oversee the Government's first forays into amplifying the capabilities of humans. Piotr wasn't sure how many months it had been exactly.

He turned and looked at the team behind him with their blue uniforms, devices at the ready. A tranquillity washed over him, like he didn't need to worry about the future anymore. It was his own machine, but testing the new Simulator was infinitely more important than the cognitive realignment surgeries he used to perform. These people had interviewed him, asked him questions he didn't know the answers to. They were keen to take down every detail of his multi-level vision, even when it became harder for him to remember. They assured him the information from his final simulation loop would be the last to fade. When they understood his memory was dying, they consoled him. They laughed and cried with Piotr, thanked him, and promised that their work would honour him.

In a few more weeks, Piotr Woyzeck wouldn't remember them either. His mind was decaying from the endless simulation loops he'd subjected it to. He trusted his team to do the test right this time, start slow, scale it up nationally, and find a way to use what was now being called organic AI. They said the project was for the benefit of everyone.

Piotr thought the woman who was Test Subject Number Eight looked like someone he knew. She was pretty. A relative? Someone from back in Poland? He hadn't been back for so long. Piotr sat in the leather chair in the sterile room and one of the members of his staff passed him his medication and a beaker of water. 'Here you are, Mr Woyzeck.'

He took the pill and returned to observing the ten subjects through the glass.

'Piotr, remember why you're doing this,' said the pretty test subject with greying hair and the onset of crows feet. 'Think of cherries, the orchards, the fallout in Wa—.' The sound from the intercom cut out before he could hear the end of what she said. He wasn't sure if he liked cherries. He'd have to go and look at his folders of notes where his memories were recorded. Although the woman could not see him, she obviously knew he was there, behind the glass.

Piotr stood and walked the length of the observation room a few times. He took the portable control panel with him. Nobody intervened or tried to stop him. In the quiet of the moment, he searched through the archives of his mind for where he knew her from. Looking into the examination room, he watched the ten people, some standing, arguing with the technicians. One of the recliners had been knocked over. He didn't hear a word of what was said. While he waited, he tapped his signet ring on the metal case of the console in his hands.

It didn't matter he wouldn't be present for the full duration of the trials. He'd already lived it, seen the results and applied them to the next set of test subjects. It would be his name people mentioned when they talked about the discovery of organic AI, but before long, he'd remember nothing of the past or the present. He would live only in distant potential futures.

Piotr studied the connections and display lights on the control panel with great intensity. He set the parameters to allow for maximum visual amplification, but only for a microsecond. He wondered which test subject could be trained to potentialise fastest. Perhaps it would be the tattooed girl or the woman who had talked about cherries.

A member of staff in a blue coat touched Piotr on the arm and guided him back to the leather chair. His mind calmed, as if his thoughts were floating. He thought he heard a distant voice saying something about stopping the test. Piotr looked through the glass and saw the ten subjects fading from view. An image of rows of cherry trees heavy with fruit washed over his mind. It was familiar somehow. As it began to dissolve, Piotr raised his hand and said, 'Begin.'

Beautiful Destruction

The glass gives way and cascades onto the driver's seat. A shard sticks into the backrest. His backrest. The windshield took six or seven or eight blows with the shovel, but it worked. I catch my breath, hands on knees, and when I straighten up to assess my handiwork, the car looks like it's asking for more — a cocky fighter with all his teeth punched out.

There's no alarm and nobody around to wince at the crashes and thuds. At least this way I can report it vandalised and get it towed the fuck out of here. I can't believe it's taken me this long to figure out how to get it gone.

I move around the car and put the windows out with the shovel blade. *Ping. Ping. Crunch.* Then I get in a few licks on the doors, too. God it feels good. Years of tension snapped in just a few minutes. The clang of metal on metal and the splinter of broken glass. I'm not sure if the smell of blood is from my own nostrils or elsewhere. My forearms tremble with the impact of each blow, muscles being torn apart, hit by hit. I drop the shovel to the ground and listen. *What you got to say about that?* The night trembles. Not even the chirp of a cricket. I breathe in and out, steadying my heart, soothing my forearms with a touch.

Destruction feels so good I go out the next night and smash another car that wasn't good enough. This one wasn't his, it's just another piece of trash that won't be moved on. When you start looking, you see it everywhere, rotten junk that people just accept for what it is. It looks a lot better with some cuts and bruises on it. For the next one, I bring a hammer and a tire iron to work a pickup into shape. Emergency surgery removes its good-for-nothing mirrors and busted tail lights, like cutting off a withered arm.

When I get back to the trailer, the crickets screech in chorus and I sleep like a child.

Soon, I'm taking a toolbag on my nightly trips — gloves, hammers, a brick and a crowbar. I even buy a steel bat from the sports store as if I'm a vigilante looking for sleeping perps to bring to justice. I free bikes from their chains and leave them to die in peace in the woods. Rusted shopping carts get wire-cutter facial reconstruction and deserted warehouses work as target practice. Select a projectile, toss the rock… *crash*. I take aim at high-and-mighty windows that thought they'd never get hit. The sprinkle of glass. Another crooked smile.

People in the neighborhood complain. 'Damned kids,' they say. 'Senseless.' I agree, but inside, I disagree. Things that look ugly mean something to me. No one would restore them, love them, use them again, so they were destroyed and broken down beyond recognition. I see them. They don't pretend, they tell the truth.

The Church of Rainbow

Beyond the cracked sidewalk, and the telephone pole with layers of flyers in a rainbow of colors, and the patch of dry brown grass, there stood a ten-foot-high concrete block wall caked with dozens of coats of paint. There was a small shrine at its base, with burnt-out candles and dead flowers. One word of graffiti filled the wall, red letters on a gold background: Rejoice!

A boy in his best white shirt faced his audience. 'Took me three weeks to finish it,' said the kid, motioning to the towering word behind him. 'Used six cans of paint, but Daddy don't miss one off his truck every few days.' He tailed off and fanned himself with a handful of posters. 'So now, we may rejoice.'

The Monson twins looked back at the boy, who stood on two palettes. They were too young to read the posters he'd drawn, perhaps too young to even understand the word rejoice. Shannon-Lee air-traced the outline of the mighty word with a stubby finger.

On the opposite side of the field, Rainbow sat with her head cocked, listening to the shouts coming from the swimming hole beyond the trees. The shimmering heat made her rust-colored coat bend and move. Rainbow came here to lie under the shade of the wall when she got tired of chasing rats in the junkyard. When the kid found her resting there one day, he decided it would be a good position for a summer vacation church. And like that, the two most important things in his life united.

'It means give praise and thanks to the creator,' said the boy. 'Jesus decreed the kingdom of God belongs to children, so why should we have to go to some grown-up church?' He stretched his arms up to the sky, as if summoning rain and began his chant. 'We will rejoice, oh yes we will.' He said this over and over again, starting slow then increasing like a satellite gaining speed in orbit. His hands gripped the makeshift pulpit and his torso whipped and whirled with the power of the phrase.

The girls copied, swinging and swaying. Mandy-May stumbled and nearly fell to the ground.

The crack of a rifle shot from the junkyard sent Rainbow running to the wall for cover. The group scattered. Uncle Steve was 'testing range'. He sure loved to hunt even though he said all the good deer in Panther Swamp had been snatched by out-of-towners. The only boar left in the woods were scrawny and fast. The kid was no expert on these matters, but he knew enough to steer clear of any Bryce family member who brought guns or bottles to the house. Steve usually brought both. He grabbed Rainbow by the collar and drew her close. Her advanced age had tempered her, made her less mean than the other Bryce dogs, who barked at anything near the junkyard in return for hambones and scraps.

If Steve was over, there might be a meal. So long as the kid fished out enough working batteries and auto parts from the duds that found their way to the Bryce yard, he could do as he pleased during vacation. But his parents, who went out all day, didn't leave much food in the house.

He and Rainbow walked over the stream, through the hole in the chain-link fence and past row upon row of part-stripped pickups. Some of them were twice as old as the kid, maybe even three times. However long he stayed, he'd never be older than the metal in the yard.

When he got back from his 'sermon', his momma asked him where he'd been. The kid said 'around', which passed for an answer at his house. The way people talked around the city was imprecise, and no one asked difficult questions. That's why the kid was called 'the kid'. He had no brothers and sisters, so it didn't matter what his name was or wasn't. Fact was he came from the Bryce clan. They were known well enough around the swamp to make him the least important of all of them.

There was no food and Uncle Steve and his daddy had already geared up and gone into the woods. The kid didn't like deer meat but ate what he was given. Sometimes there was beans or stew. Without a nearby store, the only source of food was from locals. Janice, the pastor's daughter, brought candies and chips when she was able to sneak out and ride the two miles to the junkyard after dark.

The kid went to the garage, where he slept during the hot summers. Although he'd never had his own room in the house, he liked the old garage and knew every inch of it. The mattress in there was mostly fine, and Rainbow could bed down with him. She was not an inside dog. The kid set down a dish of water he'd made from an old hubcap and ruffled the fur on her head. While he talked about how he planned to leave town and spread the word of the Gospel, the dog drank her water and listened. He recited verses from the Bible as the bright strip light shone gold over the dust motes.

While he waited for the hunters to return, the kid handled his collection of old car badges. He liked engines enough, but it wasn't his passion, not like his daddy, who looked through black and white automobile magazines and pressed his ear to the hood of twenty-year-old trucks to hear them tick over. With no sound but the distant evening cicada drone, he hummed some of the songs they sang at church. 'Sunday's a way away,' said the kid to Rainbow, who was curled up on the mattress. He studied the stack of posters he'd given out at the swimming hole. They read *Panther Swamp Summer Church. 4 pm service, behind Bryce Yard.* He'd added a note about free drinks at the bottom. Should he change 'yard' to 'automobile reclamation' like his daddy told folks in Yazoo? On Sunday, when the family wore shirts and rode in the good truck to town, he would tell the Pastor about his new church.

To his mind, the kid had already completed his mission of building a church from scratch — one where he could attend every day and where he wasn't shoved to the back and told to be quiet. He had made his leaflets, painted a sign, and created a pulpit of sorts. Some of the children who came past his property to get to the swimming hole listened while he chanted and practised his moves, leaping around like he was preaching to thousands, feeding off their summer energy. As he turned the pages of the Book of Matthew, a line reached out and grabbed him by the collar. It said '*From the lips of children and infants you, Lord, have called forth your praise.*' The kid scanned it again, then read it aloud to Rainbow. He stood and delivered the line as he'd seen Pastor Michael do in the Baptist church on Sundays. The other children might not go back to swimming so quickly if he could use this book to tell them they were calling the shots now. This truly was a moment to rejoice. The path ahead sharpened and crystalised with each pure line he found. He took a glass bottle of root beer from the corner of the garage. It felt cool to the touch and he pressed it to his cheek. Before he prised the top off, he held it up to the strip light and observed the reds and browns dance in the bottle. He took a plastic cup from one of the shelves, blew off the dust and poured himself a cup.

For the next hour, he sat cross-legged on the mattress with a pencil and paper in hand, copying any passages he could apply to his radical new philosophy that children should teach themselves about the Bible.

He took a sip of root beer each time he found something worth noting down. When his hunger overpowered his focus, the kid took the push bike that leant on the far wall and lifted Rainbow into the fraying basket. They rode to the dumpsters at the end of the lot where richer folks threw their trash. In one of the dumpsters, the kid found two pizza boxes with all the crusts still intact. He tucked the boxes under his arm and rode home with Rainbow in the basket. When he got back, there was much to study.

The screeching sound of the metal door inching up snapped the kid's concentration. Silhouettes of the boy's father and Uncle Steve blocked the fading light from outside. His father propped two guns against the wall and helped his brother lower the carcass from his shoulders to the ground.

'Not much eatin'. Maybe something for the hounds,' he said. 'At least with this son'bitch gone the deer got a chance.' He looked down at the lifeless grey scruff of coyote on the concrete floor and prodded it with a boot. 'You don't mind if we leave this son'bitch here do you, boy?'

The kid inspected the animal. How was he supposed to sleep with a stinking dead wolf in his room? What if anyone came over? 'Alright then,' he muttered. Steve nodded righteously and they headed through the front door to get cleaned up. Rainbow eyed the corpse, wary of getting too close. The kid went back to writing his manifesto and left the garage door open to let the cooling air in, and the smell of dead coyote out.

A while later, the unmistakable sound of Janice's ten-speed bicycle bumped and clattered up the dirt path toward the garage. Every time she rode it, he wanted to ask her if he could swap it for the ladies bicycle in the garage. But he didn't.

'Hey, you there?' she whispered. She knew he was because she could see the light peeking out onto the drive from under the retractable door. Janice didn't wait for an answer and hauled the door up herself. She stood for a moment, her shoulder-length hair highlighted by the moon.

'Shh,' he said. 'Don't want my folks coming out here raising up trouble. You know they tell your daddy 'most everything.' He helped her in with the bike and explained that the dead coyote in the corner was nothing to be afraid of. As he stroked Rainbow he said, 'This one's just lazy.'

Janice removed a box of donuts from her bag. They were stale, but they ate some and finished the coke. As they ate, the kid closed his eyes and waited for the rush of sugar. Janice was a year older, and probably just came over because her parents told her not to mix with the junkyard family. The kid didn't mind, he was pleased to have someone to talk to apart from his old dog and the broken vehicles. He was old enough to know he found her attractive, but not old enough to do anything about it. He wrote some of her homework, fixed up her bike real nice, and showed off his little auto-part trophies and displays. If his daddy found out, he would make jokes about him being a lapdog for another girl in the neighborhood.

Janice said there was not much news from the city. There never was when school was out. So, the kid told her about his creation, his church for the kids. She smoked the cigarette the kid had found in a pack left in an old paint tin on his shelf. She listened while he talked, blowing the smoke under the garage door.

'Three ideas,' he said, 'for the Panther Swamp Church.' The kid looked around as if to check for intruders. 'No adults, period,' he said, 'and no clever twisting of the Bible's words. We just read.' He paused, waiting to see if Janice had any input, but she listened, seemingly impressed with his plan. 'Three — we get other kids to join us so we got a voice, not just suffering the consequences of all these other folks' sins.'

Janice looked into her empty cup. 'You should think of a better name,' she said. 'But, that aside, I'd like to help.' She reached for the Bible and turned to the Book of Peter. She read aloud, '*Like newborn babies, crave pure spiritual milk, so that by it you may grow up in your salvation, now that you have tasted that the Lord is good.*'

The kid looked back at the preacher's daughter with a mixture of admiration and awe. The others at the swimming hole liked his offer of free coke, and there was always enough 'spiritual milk' in the garage to go around.

Over the next few days, the numbers at his church grew. Janice distributed fliers and told the kids to be careful not to let their parents know. Turning it into some kind of secret club was fun, even if it got the

156

kids' attention for only half an hour. The free coke and ice they hauled down to the wall each day helped.

The kid never made his services sound like lectures. He asked questions and had a quote ready for every answer. He spoke with assurance, not arrogance. The weather remained hot, and by the end of the week, numbers increased to twelve. The others, who had ignored the kid throughout the school year as the least important junkyard Bryce, took to his readings. Their parents didn't mind them being 'around', and there was little entertainment other than swimming. They joined in with whoops and hollers of 'we will rejoice,' while the kid preacher danced his whirling dance on the palettes. Afterwards, they tossed their empty cups and plunged themselves back into the cool waters of the swimming hole.

It was the Sunday service in Yazoo before anyone over the age of eighteen knew about the new preacher in town. Jeremy Gates yammered a little too loudly about free drinks and Bible dancing. His momma overheard. She was a curious type, but, she said at least it was better than throwing rocks at abandoned houses.

The service went slow and the searing August sun burned down with fire and brimstone on the wooden church building. Most of the congregation didn't have much desire to sing and clap and shout their amens. They near melted into their chairs that day.

When it finished, the kid pitched fastball questions at Pastor Michael. How do you know if you have what it takes to preach? How old is old enough? Does he have any advice?

The preacher itched to get back to his air-conditioned apartment in town. 'It ain't a choice, young'un. You've got to know the Good Book inside out, and apply the teachings.' He looked down at the kid and put on his most godly voice. 'Preaching is a calling, but you also need the authority of the Lord. Otherwise, y'all just have a cult.'

This wasn't the answer the kid had hoped for. Why didn't the pastor say where he got *his* divine authority? Were licences earned like high school diplomas? He focussed on the pastor's motorcycle boots and nodded gravely.

Out in the truck, his momma and daddy looked mighty uncomfortable in their Sunday suits. 'Where you been, boy? This truck's a goddamn oven.' The kid apologised and told them he'd been conversing with the pastor about how to serve God. His daddy told him fixing cars was easier than righting sins. At least motor vehicles didn't talk back. His momma laughed and touched his daddy's arm. The kid didn't see anything funny.

The next Monday, the kid read the congregation Ephesians 2, verses 8 and 9: *For by grace are ye saved through faith ... not of works.* On Tuesday, nearly twenty kids heard him quote the Book of James, saying '*by works a man is justified, and not by faith only*'. 'This book's full of contradictions those dumb adults don't notice,' he said to much applause and laughter. Some of them called it the Church of Rainbow, because of the colorful posters on the wall and the dog that now sat on the podium with its owner. 'The youth of Mississippi deserve a voice. We will rejoice, oh yes, rejoice!'

As the kid lay on the mattress in the garage, writing down some phrases for what would be his penultimate sermon at his summer church, he heard raised voices coming from the stoop. Rainbow stirred from her new sleeping spot where the coyote carcass had once lain. 'What's he done now?' said the voices, '... well, that ain't right... yes, sir, I'll tell him.' Through the crack under the retractable door, the kid saw a pair of motorcycle boots walking back up the drive and a four-cylinder engine fire into life and drive into the night. Who had told? It couldn't be Janice. The kid thought about taking the bike and running from the impending beating, but he had nowhere to go. Besides, who would look after Rainbow if he wasn't there to feed her pizza crusts and donuts?

After it was over, his back burned hot. That was where the studded belt had done most of the damage. His hands and arms screamed with the pain and humiliation of a hundred blows. Penance for his sins, his daddy said. Rainbow had tried to intervene, but after a few blows she cowered in the corner too. Screws and bolts and miscellaneous auto badges had flown off the shelves and clattered onto the floor. Later on, the kid replayed the one-sided shouting match about respecting the Baptist way and knowing his place, and decided that he wouldn't need a sermon tomorrow after all.

There weren't many children at the swimming hole the next day. Pastor Michael had warned them too. The Monson twins came, and the other few that turned up were high-schoolers. Janice wasn't there. The kid did not wear his best shirt that day, nor did he wear any shirt. He showed the wounds that his father and by proxy the entire congregation of the Yazoo Baptist Church had inflicted. Angry red sores and welts on his scrawny back. Bright indigo-green bruises on his forearms, and a violet black eye — all the colors of the spectrum.

'This is what becomes of those who seek change,' he said. 'Even though we are the owners of this good kingdom.' The teenagers watched from a distance. The kid continued. 'We'll go back to school next week to learn how to stand in line to become good citizens, but we have a voice, same as every other person in this country.' He raised his arms into the crucifix position and held the pose. The older boys had seen enough to mark him down as crazy — the junkyard preacher. As they pedalled off on their bicycles, the kid shouted after them. 'And that voice says rejoice. Yes it does.'

Beyond the cracked sidewalk, and the telephone pole with layers of flyers in a rainbow of colors, there stood a ten-foot-high concrete block wall caked with dozens of coats of paint. The one word, Rejoice, which took three weeks to paint, and which filled the wall, had been covered. Its red and gold letters were masked by fliers for the Yazoo Baptist Church, which boasted of community spirit and free music. The pulpit was gone. Smashed up and taken. In front of the small shrine, lay the lifeless rust-colored carcass of a dead dog. Her head was flat and broken. Her eyes framed the bullet hole. The Church of Rainbow was his idea, not hers. She lay stiller than that coyote carcass.

Although Janice had betrayed his trust, the kid still loved her. He didn't know what romantic love felt like, but he loved her like Jesus loved his people. If Pastor Michael could stoop to such depths as to take the life of an old dog, then no one was free and clear from needing guidance. One of his great loves had consumed the other. The Lord had given him so much, but had also taken away. This was the God of contradiction. This was the same God that forbade people to kill, but in Exodus 32, instructed '*put a sword by the side of every man.*'

The kid was certain that he had loved Rainbow. That dog had kept him company through hours sifting through jagged metal, looking for live batteries and salvage. She kept him company writing papers in the garage. She suffered the same hot summers and the cold winters. She rejoiced in the creation of her own church, and danced and barked along with the congregation. It was over for the kid — the junkyard, the church, the whole place. When he was old enough to fix engines and spread the word of the Gospel, he'd do it far away from there. He would get a dog, a loyal friend, and he would use a new name. 'The kid' would stay in Yazoo, Mississippi.

Saudade

When Richie McManus lost his hand in the hydraulic winch, he screamed like a banshee, but the North Sea winds whipped the noise away. I was hauling in gear on the port side and the alarm light snapped me out of my own thoughts. McManus was only a few meters away on the other side of the deck. I dinnae hear a thing.

It was clean off, just above the wrist. The hand got mangled and lost in the machinery. We clamped on a tourniquet, got him onto the mess table and cleaned the wound. We heard him scream *then* all right. Brucey even ran back outside to throw up. The galley was usually quiet, but McManus shouted his fuckin' head off that night. Who wouldn't? It was a long steam back to port. Thirty-six hours of saying the same things over and over again.

'Doctors can do wonders these days, pal. Prosthetics and all. And there's jobs too for… you know.'

He looked, full stare, like he dared us to finish the thought.

Mostly we stayed quiet and watched the knots to shore tick down.

People sometimes ask us why we get paid so well. Richie's accident was why. Chances are we'd all have a lapse in concentration at some point. Every fisherman leaves something out there, whether it's the best years of his life or his right hand. For once, none of the crew was thinking about the taste of that first pint in the Angus Arms, or the first leg-up they'd get.

I took a shift sitting up with him. After the shock died, the colour in his face started to come back, but outside it was black. We listened to the force seven ripping the ocean apart and watched the spray batter the glass of the navigation bridge. Four long hours.

During the sunrise, I changed the dressing. The gauze was stuck to his wrist, with an ugly bit of bone exposed. By then, McManus had used up all our painkillers. He winced as I fixed a new dressing, biting through his teeth. He calmed once it was done. We followed the dark horizon, looking for other vessels. Nothing there.

'Yous ever heard about that Portuguese word?' he asked after a while. '*Saudade.*'

'Nah. No idea, pal.'

'*Saudade.* Aye, it's one of those words withoot a translation. Comes from their nautical culture.'

I turned to face him, keeping my eyes well away from his wound. 'What's it mean then?'

He straightened up in his seat. 'It's like a longing. You know, missing something.'

I inhaled on a cigarette I didn't have. Longing. 'Like a gut feeling?'

'Aye, kind'ae. A feeling of not knowin'. Families not knowin' when sailors will be back. Or if...' He looked as the first light cast its golden net over the sea. The winds had all but died. 'Sort of like love and loss all at once.'

The Portuguese have the whole bastard Atlantic to stare at, I thought. I packed away the medical kit.

'I think aboot it on these weeks away. The water holds you at arm's length from your life, you know?'

I did. We all did. Going back to shore was okay for a few days, then you got that craving to go back out, never at peace.

'Been doing this seventeen years,' he said, 'and now's the first time I haven'ae felt it.'

'Felt what?'

'That *saudade* thing.' He held up his ruined arm as if thanking it for setting him free.

When we docked, Skip took him straight to the hospital to get seen. All six of us visited him the next day. His family were philosophical about it, not angry. McManus knew all Skip had was a battered trawler, and traders were squeezing us on the price of prawn anyhow. No point in suing.

Soon as we knew he was okay, we wanted to find a replacement and get back out there. It was peak season and we'd earned next to nothing on the trip. Skip suggested we wait a week out of respect.

So I went back to Aberdeen and told Aileen we'd have to cut some expenses over the summer. My wife only knew McManus in passing, but the news affected

165

her. 'Poor man, his poor family,' she kept saying. 'We ought to be thankful.'

'Aye, hen.'

We kissed and it was a real kiss. Not a protocol peck on the lips like usual. When I drew back and looked at her, my arms still anchored around her neck, I just about cried. Being away was hard and being back was harder. Never able to be in one place or the other. That kiss told her how much I loved her and wee Donny more than saying it ever could.

Our boy was on his school camp, so the old house was calm. Those few days without him, it echoed and creaked like an ageing vessel. I plugged a few draft holes and fixed a dripping tap, then shipped out again the next Saturday.

I suppose that's why we dinnae call it home. It's shore. It's land. But the sea isn't home either. You cannae own it, you can only own a piece of the space between the two.

McManus got a delivery job, which is sort of the opposite of catching fish when you think about it. I told him that, but he dinnae get it. He still drinks in the Angus Arms, only with his left hand now.

'Yous lot are welcome to the prawn,' he said, when we saw him after the season. 'I dinnae miss it a bit.'

We all eyed each other, disbelieving, but he meant it. We'd only just got ashore but our minds were still tethered to the dark waters and white spray of the North Sea. And there he was, sitting with a glass of single malt and a grin on his face.

Windows Explorer Cannot Process This Request

*A*re you sure you want to reopen this application?
[Yes] X [No]

C:\Users\Steve\Business\Tax Returns\2017-18

I loved your efficiency; you laughed at my buy-now-pay-later attitude. How did you tally £19,446.40 in expenses even though you never spent more than ten pounds at the barbers? You even drove everywhere in fourth gear to save fuel. Your final email was to the Inland Revenue, not me. That hurts.

C:\Users\Steve\Documents\xmaslist17

You left gift idea documents for me to find, as if each item had an invisible question mark. On the 25th, we held hands on the heath and all the questions got left there. A few months later, you went to ground — secret Santa sneaking back to hibernate in his Lapland lair.

D:\Photos\Holidays\St.Tropez\Edited

You always were good at cropping things out of your life. Cutting and pasting one credit card for another. On our one-year anniversary you put your hands around my throat while we made love. I let you squeeze harder than I wanted. After, I took your photo as you stood on the balcony, surveying your kingdom. That one's not in the folder. It's just smiles, sunsets and pictures of far-off yachts.

E:\Removable Device\Marriage Certificate.pdf
   [This archive is corrupted]
   Did you plan your escape before or after the vows? In overdraft and in debt. Can't divorce a missing person; now I'm married to your faulty numbers.

C:\System32\vectors\beta\properties
   Solid detective work led me to your carefully hidden porn. Clicking into every folder took hours. There's nothing incriminating here, just stills of women trapped in compromising positions.

Locked Folder C:\Users\Steve\OperationSunset
   Do you get a kick out of imagining the repeated 'access denied' message? Caribbean destinations, tentatively chosen child names, thriller titles, clues from the half-finished Times crossword — nothing works. The computer expert I hired couldn't unlock the real you either.

I've gone through all the stages, wept, cut your poisonous plastic cards into tiny pieces. All that's left of you to explore is this PC and I won't stop until I crack the code. Until I find you. When I do, I'll wrap my hands around your throat, and I'll ask 'why?'.

Are you sure you want to create the file 'Steven's Funeral?'

The Matchstick House

They sit cross-legged on the carpet, sixteen little faces with mismatched red and blue uniforms. Some of them are barefoot.

'Good morning, children,' I say in English.

Two of the boys chatter in Nepali. They hit children for less in my old school.

'I said *good morning*, everybody.'

'Good morning teacher,' they chant, half-heartedly. Tomorrow is Saturday and they won't be in school. Dinesh is late as usual. He enters while I take the register. His uniform is dirty. Many of the children come from fractured homes and Dinesh has not learned to wash his clothes.

'Dinesh.'

He stops in his tracks and looks at me as if he has no idea how or why he is late.

'Tell me what we talked about yesterday and then you may sit.'

He sits down immediately and the class laughs. One of the girls comments that he must be stupid. He needs to work on his listening is all.

'Tell me *first*, then you may sit.'

'Oh,' he stutters, scrambling to his feet, 'work. Jobs.'

'Very good,' I say with an encouraging glance. 'What you might want to do when you are a grown up.'

A hand shoots up in the front row. 'Your calling,' says Neema, without waiting to be chosen. She turns to Dinesh. 'Stupid people don't have a calling.'

It will be difficult to switch the children's focus to mathematics today. Neema's test scores are high, but she could use some of the emotional intelligence as Dinesh has. 'Very well,' I say. 'I will prove to you that every person on this planet has a calling. Would you like to hear a story?'

Emphatic agreement.

I give each pupil a board, a pencil and a piece of paper, and I begin the task. 'I'll tell you about a pupil of mine from some years ago. She was exactly your age when she first came to the academy.' Our privately-funded school was very different back then, but in just twelve years, it has grown to offer more than one hundred children a free education at any one time. 'Remember to write notes about what I tell you. Write how it makes you feel.'

While I do not make a habit of giving long speeches to the children, I tell each of my classes about this amazing girl, years after she left my care. 'Her name was Jhoti. It was the only word she could write. You see, she had several disabilities such as palsy of movement and an inability to speak. She was different.' In truth she was a cruelly deformed girl with gaps between her teeth, and a jerking style of movement. Her brain development had been impaired when in vitro.

Neema asks if she was like Omesh, a boy at school who has Down's Syndrome. I tell the class she had a disability, but a different one to Omesh.

Some of them roll the word around their mouths, practising. 'Disability.'

'She could not make friends or play. She could not run or read or sing like all of you. Jhoti lived on her own in an abandoned house outside of the village. Apart from some clothes, and what food the villagers gave, the only possession she had was a miniature house made out of little pieces of wood.'

Many of the children have favourite toys like plastic action figures or little trinkets they collect. These things are more common in Nepal now. Yet the matchstick house Jhoti carried with her was beautifully crafted. Hundreds of tiny pieces of wood meticulously cut, glued together and framed with neat red borders. Its roof slanted, and its front door and little windows invited you to look inside. Only the people were missing.

'Jhoti could not focus on many class activities, but she cared deeply about that house. She would stare at it, concentrate on it, protect it from harm. She put the difficulties of her life inside it, and kept them locked in there.'

The class are now silent and still. Even Dinesh listens carefully. Their papers contain marks and notes. Some have written the girl's name or the word 'disability'. Two children in the centre of the small classroom are drawing the matchstick house.

'Although she could not speak, Jhoti learned to communicate with signs.' I practice a few of the signs with the students — hungry, tired, mountains, happy. They take this part very seriously.

'Her classmates were curious about the matchstick house and where she found it. They did not ask to touch it, because they knew how important it was to Jhoti.'

Teaching Jhoti could be frustrating, but we bonded over a love of our part of the world. During break times, we would stand and stare at the Annapurna range across the valley from our school. Lines of razor-sharp ridges and the clear blue sky. We enjoyed the air, dry and cool. 'She loved the mountains and the animals that call them home. She would point, she would smile and feel the elements of the landscape.'

Truly we are blessed in Gaunshahar. Villages rest on the hillsides as though the gods themselves sprinkled them from up high. Little puffs of woodsmoke rise. The sunrise beams pinks and oranges across the land. Oxen work the fields of rice and corn.

'Jhoti came to school for six months, and every day, as she walked home carrying her matchstick house, she would stop and look at the horses on Sunil Pradesh's farm. It took hours to reach her house.' I spoke to my wife about taking the girl in. Jhoti needed help and guidance and we had a two-storey house and

174

a vehicle. Villagers whispered that her mother was a drunkard who caused the fire which burned the village's livestock.

'Then, one day,' I continue, 'Jhoti did not come to school. Nor the next day, nor the one after that.'

One of the children asks if she died.

'No,' I say. 'She took her clothes and left the village with her little matchstick house. Even though it was very difficult for her to walk far, no one knew where she was.'

I could not help feeling responsible for the girl and took the Jeep to look for her. I asked in the villages around, but to no avail. A big town can be a scary place for a nine-year-old, especially with all of her disadvantages. The nights were cold and if she did not find shelter, she might die.

'The next Sunday, I made the trip again to Besisahar.' The town is a day's walk from our village. It is where the tourists begin their walks into the Annapurna. 'Only in this second week of searching, did I find Jhoti.'

The children's eyes glaze. Finally, they sit still, captivated, following Jhoti's story, trying to see things from this girl's perspective.

'Besisahar can be a dangerous place. Trucks belch out black fumes and stray dogs fight for scraps on the dusty street. There are robbers. Would you like to know where I found her?'

They wag their heads up and down.

'On the outskirts of the town, sleeping in a stable.'

From the corner of my eye, I see Dinesh smile, as if he recognises something in the story.

The owner had tried, unsuccessfully, to remove her. He told me he had shouted, kicked her, told her to find somewhere else to sleep, but she was drawn to the place and slept on the straw with the horses. She had with her a little orange kitten which she fed. It followed her and slept on the straw. She treated it with a softness of movement I didn't think her capable of.

A few students' hands raise. One asks, 'Did she still have the house?'

'Yes. It was still with her, unharmed.' It was more important for her to care for that pile of matchsticks than it was for her to look after herself. 'I took her back to the village and she came to live with my family. She brought her cat and her matchstick house with her.'

As time went by, Jhoti became part of our family. My twelve-year-old son Manish was a wonder. When he returned from his schooling in Besisahar, he showed a kindness that made me swell with pride. Countless hours, they worked on her signing and fine-motor skills. She was still restless, but before long, she could communicate her needs better. With a more balanced diet of fruits and *dal bhaat*, her physical condition improved. 'Jhoti became a part of my family because her own had deserted her.' Anything she received, she offered to share. When good people need help they still give as well as take. That's emotional intelligence.

'All right, children,' I say, 'it's time for an activity.' I ring the class bell and begin to write on the board. 'You remember what Jhoti's most precious object was?'

'The matchstick house,' they call out, almost in unison.

'Good. Now you must write down what your treasured possession is and why.' I give them three minutes and sit on the carpet with them to check their papers. The results are always fascinating. We do not have much material wealth, and some of these children have not even seen the way people live in Kathmandu or Pokhara.

One by one, the children go to the front of the class and write their objects on the board — sunglasses, a family photo, their chickens, a mobile telephone, dried flowers from the November festival. Most of them can't justify their choice, they just like it, but some of the pupils are able to explain who gave it to them or what it represents. Dinesh talks about a pair of donated football boots. They allow him to run faster, turn quicker and score more goals for his team. They allow him to dream.

'Let's continue with the story.' I take my place, standing at the front. 'Doctors in the city told us her condition could not be improved. Without any official documents, she was not able to receive treatment for free. In the years she spent at this school and with my family, we saw her character — independent, caring, and strong. She refused to sit on chairs and disliked being inside too long. She would walk between the villages to be among the birds, the horses and cows, all the while cradling her matchstick house.' At times I didn't know if she was protecting the house, or if it protected her.

My wife and I had many conversations about what would happen when Jhoti reached adulthood. By the age of twelve, she could not attend the school of which I was principal, and we had no legal guardianship. She could never be married. She was a child lost in the system, with no paperwork and no rights. Everyone deserves their own life. She understood how to approach animals, how to handle them, and how to care for their needs. Her orange cat grew large and confident, and the horses down the hill on Sunil Pradesh's farm approached when they saw her. The furthest we got to discovering what happened with her family was that there was a fire. When we talked of her past, she would cry and stare for hours at her matchstick house, stroking its contours and following its lines. In the evenings she sat by the big tree at sunset, holding the thing up to the light and peering inside, as if checking that her miniature world was still alive and well.

'So, where do you think Jhoti is now?' I ask.

Some of the children frown. All they know of home is the earth and the skies of our village. Their houses and the school are the borders of their worlds.

'Now, she has a job near Pokhara.' Since the age of fourteen, she has lived in a stable run by a second cousin of mine, near to the city. 'Jhoti is sixteen. She grooms the horses, cleans the stables and organises the equipment. She meets many tourists, who ride the horses up into the Himalaya. This life is her calling.'

The first break is approaching, and the children's minds wander towards feeling the sun on their skin, and dancing and playing football in the playground. Most of them have abandoned their pencils and paper, but Dinesh is finally writing.

'Before you go outside, I want to show you one thing.'

The three girls in the front row light up. They will be the first to see. I unlock my desk drawer and carefully remove the matchstick house. 'This is now *my* most treasured possession, children. Jhoti gave this to me when she left for the stables. Pass it round very carefully.'

I hand it to Neema and she seems surprised that such a basic toy could have entertained someone for years. After a few seconds, she passes it to the next child. 'Remember, this girl could not speak, she could not communicate well or write, but when she left, she gave my family her most valuable possession. Along with the tears of our goodbye, it was all she could leave us to keep our spirits connected.

Neema raised her hand. 'And she can visit you anytime she wants?'

'Yes,' I say. 'But she has her own life now, her calling.'

Dinesh, who has been staring out of the window for these last few minutes finally gets his chance to look at the object. He stares in through the door, just as Jhoti used to, perhaps wondering what happened to all of the trouble and difficulty she kept locked inside it for years.

'Very good,' I say. 'You don't want to miss your turn playing football. Go outside and play.

Dinesh rushes to the door and gets there ahead of his classmates. 'Thank you,' he shouts. The children try to squeeze through at the same time and spill out into the playground.

As I collect the papers, I am pleased to see Dinesh has written something on his: *Everyone has a calling. Others can help you find it.* My face glows. My chest swells. Next time I tell the story, I may use this line. I collect the boards, the pencils and the papers on the floor and return the matchstick house to its drawer.

The Anatomy of a Hurdy-Gurdy

The curve of the body is yours. Wooden lines flow and breathe. I cradle you, as if you are still a part of me, but you are not. My hurdy-gurdy is perfectly rounded, yet with angular interruptions. Its rough edges wear smooth through years of repetitions. Diners at long tables watch the instrument, not me. My best clothes would not count among their worst. I blend into the stone walls. That one night, you watched *me* and we listened to each other's breath and heartbeat as if it were an orchestra.

I turn the handle and begin; the banquet conversation does not hush. Most continue their own drone and melody. The wheel runs crooked, its motion impure. My arm turns the handle in perfect muscle memory and the cracked wheel travels around. The beating I received was your husband's muscle memory. I didn't know you were married, or that it would be impossible to play for three months with broken hands. Eventually, the wheel turned again and the people danced, but the sound was never the same.

Within the bridge lies peculiar tension. The luthier says that one day it will snap, like the back of a labourer carrying some great load. For now, I play and the strings sing sweet lies, just as you did to me.

The keys dance up and down in tune. Ivory teeth constructing their story of good and evil. The lord catches the moment my fingers stray onto a wrong note. One lapse is all it takes to be cast out. I play for an hour but I have slipped. I have fallen, just as the very instrument did, from the cathedral to the dining hall. Soon, this banquet will end. All that will be left are bowls filled with splintered bones and apple cores.

The protective case shuts over another performance and the players take to the stage. Eyes closing, yet sleep will not come. The guests will dance in merriment. Not I. Cracks in polished wood rarely show from a distance. I am an expert at putting my instrument back together, piece by piece, straightening the pegs and changing rusty strings as if nothing happened. But, once broken, a wheel never runs true.

Triple Word Score

We've never had a playoff before. The first match finished in a draw, so I reset the board and they'll start again. I'd usually be fast asleep by now, but I'm here, officiating in front of a hundred people as the rank outsider, Mikkael Iliescu takes on seven-time champion, Norman White. For White, it's all about the Association of British Scrabble Players title, but for Mikkael, the cash prize would be life changing.

Members of the crowd crane their necks for a better look. They switch their view from the players to the big screen as if the tiles might change. The screen shows the game board, with its wonderful words criss-crossing each other: *solarium, banshee, gherkins, quern, pesticide, formulae*. The tournament competitors have stayed to see if the first-time finalist can beat the greatest player the game has ever seen. We're not supposed to pick sides, but I have a son named Michael. His family live in Australia now. I don't see them much. I don't see anyone much, then *bam*, it's the UK Open again. Mikkael runs through his combinations, his eyes wide, flitting between rack and board. Norman considers the words through his thick-framed glasses.

You get strange sorts here, etymological nerds and lexical know-it-alls, although they don't utter many words. I'd describe most of the players as *reclusive*: fourteen points. Can I do better than fourteen? *Misanthrope*: twenty-one. There you go. They might not be the most social bunch, but none of them are leaving until they know the result.

Running the biggest tournament in Europe is hard work for a codger like me, but I always look forward to meeting the competitors on the first weekend in October. Since Helen passed, it's just me and the dog. I must say, in my twenty years of judging, I've never seen a competitor like Mikkael. He's encyclopedic, oddly specific, obsessed, and has the look of a bird who just found an impostor in its nest. Fifty years ago, I was him, playing in my first final, gambling on winning enough pay for my bed & breakfast and ticket home.

It was Friday morning I first met Mr Iliescu. The association president, Dave, and I were hanging the banners and getting everything up to ABSP standard. Enter a pasty young man, sporting a crumpled tracksuit.

'Hello, there,' I said. 'Registration doesn't open until twelve.' I don't know what he asked for when he went to the barber, but unless it was 'the electrocuted by the toaster' look, he was getting seen off.

He emitted a high-pitched laugh. 'Oh, yes, I am cognizant of this.' Another laugh. 'My autobus just dismounted.'

184

Quite the vocabulary on this one. I enquired where he had travelled from.

'I'm from Transylvania, in Romania.' The Sesame Street Dracula doll attached to the zip of his rucksack seemed to back this up.

'Oh. I'm not sure we've had a Romanian player before. Did you fly to London or Birmingham?'

His laugh was a little nervous this time. 'Eh, no. I arrived presently, on a bus. From Romania.' No wonder he looked like he had slept in a bunker. My goodness. I only came eight miles, and I still felt bleary eyed. 'It took forty-two hours, seventeen minutes, and twenty seconds,' he said.

'Well, welcome to the UK Open. I'm Warren Parr.' I proffered a hand.

'Mikkael,' he said, as another titter escaped. 'Pleased to acquaint you. It is my inaugural tournament here.' He smiled, perhaps dreaming of the prize money, and revealed an upper incisor so crooked it appeared to be attempting a jailbreak.

While I dressed tables and coordinated with hotel staff, Mikkael crouched on the floor (rather than using the chairs provided) and alternated between nearly nodding off and leafing through the Official Scrabble Players' dictionary after jolting awake. It's amazing that someone could sit on a bus for two days and not want to get some fresh air. Then again, there's not much to see in Coventry.

The first day was hectic. More Scrabblers enter every year, but our team is just me and Dave with the occasional help from his missus. I shouldn't complain, it's our marquee event, and all the big names come to town. I still hold out hope of seeing one of the top scoring words in live play: *quixotry, quizzify, muzjinks, oxazepam, syzygy*. One day.

As you get older, you notice the players getting younger. This year's lot sported spiky haircuts and clothes which didn't fit properly. They rushed around, fixated on electronic gizmos. I hobbled from table to table with my stick.

After scribbling down the scores in my notebook, I inputted them to the computer, which displayed the next matches on the leaderboard. It was my job to ensure we were on schedule. Dave just swanned around shaking hands with other association chiefs and interested bystanders. On top of my duties, I fielded questions from the players.

'Are Blank Bingos permitted under ABSP rules?'

'How many copies of OSPD4 do you have in the break area?'

'My opponent has been *brailing*. Can I lodge an official complaint?'

Most of the guys (and they are mostly men) weren't socially apt. They could pluck the most obscure Victorian vocabulary from a pool of jumbled up letters, yet they could barely string two words together. When I could, I followed the progress of our Transylvanian wanderer. He won his preliminaries and accrued a decent points differential.

During the breaks, the players went outside to make calls, stretch their legs, and consume a variety of brightly coloured drinks. Not Mikkael. He seemed allergic to natural light and clung to the lobby. He spent his break typing feverishly into a tiny laptop computer, chattering away to himself. It was like he was some kind of calculator, having to verbally process the gobbledygook he was inputting — complex algorithms and incomprehensible script, no doubt. At lunch he sat alone, switching his focus from his computer screen to his dinner plate. Helen used to say food tastes better with company. As always, she was right. I headed over.

He smiled nervously, revealing the tooth that popped out at a forty-five-degree angle. 'Hello again, Mr. Warren. Today is very spectacular.'

'You had a successful morning, Mikkael.'

'Yes, my objective is to proliferate to the next round,' he replied with a bulging mouth. His plate struggled under the weight of pasta salad, potato salad, a crisp mountain and sandwich triangles. Two glasses of milk stood guard on either side of his feast. I told him he could go back for seconds, but he said his body consumed 'astounding quantities' of carbohydrates because he ran marathons.

Over lunch he gave me his life story — university 'with only sixteen years of antiquity', parents losing their farm to the bank, and him paying for his sister's education. He laughed as he told me that the first prize of five thousand pounds would be life transforming, but I could see he didn't really find it funny.

'I work with computers. Perhaps you noticed my contraptions,' he said as if his battered laptop was the only thing on my mind.

'Some kind of coding thingy, is it?'

If only the conversation would shut down soon. I'm not technical or technological. 'End-to-end encryption', apparently. Thankfully, before he could start going into routers and HTMLs, another player joined our table.

'Err, hello,' she said. 'Did you say you're from Romania?'

Mikkael reached into his tracksuit pocket and fished out the rather grubby Dracula toy. 'Yes. Transylvania,' he said while waggling the doll. He laughed. So did the girl.

She was short with big eyes and a swept fringe, like a baby highland cow. Perhaps it was the nose ring that made me think that, although baby cows don't have as many tattoos on their arms.

'I'm Mona,' she said, 'from Bucharest. So there's two of us, I guess.' She extended her hand.

Mikkael put The Count back in his pocket and dusted off his hand. He looked at me as if he was checking he was doing it right, then shook. 'Mikkael.'

Sandwich crumbs sprayed from his mouth as he talked. That was me, an awkward eighteen year-old asking my Helen to dance for the first time. Turned out she didn't know any steps either, but we got better over time. Mikkael fished out a disposable camera from his bag, one of the little yellow ones you have to wind forward after every shot. They posed for a photo, cheek to cheek, and I pressed the button. I handed the camera back to Mikkael, and he inspected it, even though there was no way of knowing how the picture would turn out.

The afternoon went by with all sixty-four competitors exchanging wins and losses, and moving anticlockwise for their next games. There were plenty of high scores, dictionary challenges, and more than a bit of coffee-housing (talking to opponents to distract them).

At home, the dog would be getting restless, and I was ready for my tea. When you're my age, you need to rest your eyes; those little game pieces aren't easy to read. Before leaving, I checked the tournament leaderboard and as expected, Norman White, the defending champion, had wiped the floor with his opposition. The other big names had advanced, and Mikkael and Mona had both made it through to the second day's play. He still had a chance at winning the first prize. I laughed at the thought of a wealthy Mikkael, transported back in time, wearing a smart black cape and bow tie, just like his mascot. Perhaps he would be joining others for dinner, but as usual, I had to eat alone.

Owning a Fox Terrier means you don't normally need an alarm clock. I'm usually up by six, but that morning Willy woke me up twenty minutes later. After I dealt with the dog and swigged back my pills, I had a quick look through the Coventry Telegraph and was surprised to see none other than Mikkael staring back at me on page fourteen. They usually do a little feature on the tournament, which is good publicity for the association, but this time, they included a fact-file interview with three of the entrants.

The first two interviews featured Janice Hopkins, a retired school bursar, and semi-professional Deepak Chaudhary, one of the favourites. Mikkael, who looked like he'd just emerged from a bush, aimed his wild stare directly at the camera.

As much as I like a natter about 'point-balancing' and 'rack management', it's not a good idea to fraternise with the competitors. As an official, it wouldn't be right to play favourites, but I found myself openly rooting for Mikkael, imagining him taking the title and prize money back to his little village in deepest Romania. In his interview, he said that he'd only started playing a year ago 'in order to meet people', same as I did 'way back when'. If only there was a tournament this big every month, I might not be stuck talking to the dog so much. Mikkael said he'd spend the £5,000 prize buying more chickens for his grandmother's farm. There's got to be a good joke in there about 'putting all of your eggs in one basket', or 'counting your chickens'. By this time, I was unfashionably late. Get in the car and drive, man. Don't stop till you reach the Quality Hotel. It would be a tiring day — a rare social outing before my next family gathering at Christmas.

Dave, the ABSP president, had made the draw in my absence. 'I couldn't wait any longer, Woz,' he said. 'The players were getting impatient.'

I hate it when he calls me Woz. It makes me sound like the past tense — something that's been and gone. However, I noted that time had gotten the better of me.

'That's not like you, Woz. Very punctual normally.' He slid his hands into his waistcoat pockets. 'Well, White looks like he's got a straight shot to the final. Be fantastic to see him win again.'

'Mmm, it's likely,' I said. 'He won the French Masters last month, and he doesn't even speak the bloody language.' The game list paired Mikkael Iliescu with Mona, the girl from lunch. 'I'll be…'

Play started and I watched game number fourteen from a distance. Mona looked well-rested and confident, but Mikkael was a nervous wreck around her. He didn't know what to do with his hands, and he was laughing far too much. Maybe that's why I took to him; back in the days before Helen came and went, I was hopeless with girls.

Mikkael had won the first game and was up in the second. His mascot stood next to him on the table, and he gave him a little tap on the head every time he recorded a score. The board lay between them with a smattering of interesting words: *rasterize, polyglot, yankee, quilled, bechamel.* Poor old Mona wasn't having much luck and had a rack full of low-value vowels. She curled her hair with a finger between turns and distracted Mikkael by firing question after question at him. 'How long are you staying here? Are you actually a robot from the future with an inbuilt dictionary?' She teased him about his interview. 'Why do you need so many chickens?' He shuffled around in his chair, and fidgeted with The Count while he batted the questions back in his bizarre English. At one point, he spilled all of the tiles in his rack onto the floor and had to call a match official to ensure he wasn't cheating.

Players sometimes talked during matches, but with £5,000 at stake, serious competitors needed to concentrate. Mikkael impressed me by producing such impressive words despite Mona's flirting. Just when I thought he might have a panic attack because of the stress, he laid down a seven letter bingo on a triple word score: *kamikaze*. One hundred and thirty-one points. He sat back in satisfaction. 'I have sacrificed my letters for your consideration,' he said with a laugh, then he took a huge gulp from his bottle of orange drink. The game was over. They shook hands and Mikkael moved onto the next round.

Any game score over five-hundred always garners interest, and before long, players and spectators came to gawk at the finished game board. Mikkael sat with a sheepish look while others took pictures on their phones. He had finished his match before everyone else, including Norman White.

Mikkael cruised through his next match against a sixteen-year-old from Leeds, but struggled in his quarter-final, winning by just three points in the deciding game. Was it all getting too much for him? The long journey, the crowds, the language. Mona kept him company during the breaks. They became inseparable — Team Transylvania. He stole glances at her whenever he thought she wasn't looking, but more often than not, she caught him and stuck her tongue out.

Once the tournament got down to four tables, management was easier. Dave and I just had to make sure no one was feeding answers or using devices. By 4 PM, we had our four semi-finalists. Norman White would face Bernice Langdon, a repeat of last year's final, and Mikkael Iliescu would need to beat Deepak Chaudhary to reach his first ranking tournament final.

Dave's long-suffering wife arrived to take over for a few hours. I'd be asleep in my judge's chair if I didn't take time out.

When I got home, I took Willy out for his walk, but instead of enjoying the grounds of Kenilworth Castle, I found myself resting on a bench, calculating Scrabble scores for my surroundings — *balustrade, drawbridge, fiefdom*. Half an hour of plodding around in the late afternoon sun did me in. Even with the extra sleep, it had been a long day. A beep from my trouser pocket woke me from a doze. Willy nearly had a heart attack when I shouted in celebration. 'Go on Mikkael, you beauty!' He had beaten Chaudhary 360 to 332.

That's how we arrived here, to a final between a Transylvanian oddball and the greatest player in the history of association Scrabble. The first game was cagey, both players playing defensively, not wanting to leave the board open. The noise of the crowd grew and grew as they mumbled possible words, scores and tactics to each other. I had to shush them when it came down to the final tile. Mikkael had one piece left, but was unable to play and the scores stayed level. We reset the board and started again.

Will White lose? Will Mikkael win enough money to help his family and take a flight home instead of the bus? Lights from camera phones blink on and off. Mikkael flaps his tracksuit jacket to get the air circulating inside. Norman sits upright, waiting. It's 11:20 PM, but he's in no hurry. He came within one point of losing his title, but he's not flustered. He just stares through his spectacles and smoothes his beard. The crowd shuffle from foot to foot. Mikkael's complexion has changed. What was a pasty white, is now overdone fried chicken. His empty orange drink bottle rests against the chair leg.

Dave pushes the action. 'Mr Iliescu, you have thirty seconds.'

Mikkael looks to The Count for help. He's got some high-value tiles, but only two vowels. By my calculations, Mikkael needs a miracle to win. Even if he could spell *miracle*, the eleven points wouldn't do him much good. White is miles ahead. Those chickens will have to stay put.

As his time expires, he speaks. 'I want to exchange,' he says with a laugh. He's forfeited his go. The crowd whisper, some of them explaining to the casual observers what it means: a new letter and a missed turn.

His opponent smiles triumphantly, mentally pocketing the prize money. This is the first exchange in a final since... well, even I can't remember one.

Mikkael needs two miracles now. He stuffs his hand into the bag and pulls out a new tile, replacing it with his dead one. In the meantime, Norman White plays his next word: *divulge*, and goes a further twenty points into the lead because of a triple letter score. Some of the crowd start to drift into the lounge bar to catch last orders.

How is Mikkael going to find his way out of this one? I can't see what he's got, but it must be something good. It appears that he's suffered some kind of short circuit, going over the maths again and again. White has left a rogue 'S' on a triple word score. Careless. Mikkael can back-hook it to pluralise a seven letter word. He scoops up all seven tiles and lays them out along the bottom row like he's showing a pearl necklace to an interested buyer. The word is *quetzals*: a rare bird and the Guatemalan currency if I'm not mistaken. It's a *double* triple-word-score bingo. Very rare. Two hundred and eighty-four points in one turn. That's the highest word score I've ever seen! Incredible. Mikkael reaches into the bag and collects the final tiles.

But wait. Dave raises a hand. 'Infraction. Fast-bagging.'

He has to be joking. Fast-bagging is for players who don't give their opponent a chance to challenge. White knows the rules. If he thought for a second that *quetzals* was questionable, he'd have challenged. The crowd chatter turns up a notch.

'Dave. Let's not be silly now.' I pull him to one side, away from the board. 'You can't call that, you'll wipe off the biggest score we've seen.'

'It was too quick, Woz.'

'Listen,' I say, 'this kid has already got enough going against him. He was just nervous for God's sake.' I won't let Dave throw his weight around this time.

'I have the final say here.' He looks over to the reigning champion, who focuses on his tiles. 'Norman?'

White lifts his head and shrugs. He's happy to play on. He wouldn't have challenged.

Dave sighs. 'Alright, let's just hope it doesn't affect the result.' He addresses the crowd. 'No infraction. Continue the play.'

The score goes up onto the screen above the players and Mona jumps two feet in the air. The crowd bubbles with excitement, counting out scores on fingers and mumbling the word over and over again. Mikkael taps The Count on the head and exhales in relief. There's nothing more he can do now. It's over to his opponent.

White needs a bingo to win. Can he use all seven of his letters? The crowd hushes. Nobody dares check their phone or take a sip of their drink. Another twenty seconds of deep thought. I've seen White weave his magic many a time, but he must be rattled by what's just transpired. The board is still quite open, but he's only holding one vowel. It could be tricky.

The play clock is counting down. He's got fifteen seconds more. Mikkael looks close to passing out.

Suddenly, White relaxes. The corner of his mouth twitches into a smile, and we know he's got something. Will it be enough? He adds all seven of his letters to an A in the top left of the board, to form *abstract*. It scores him 74 and by finishing his letters, Mikkael's rack counts double against him. I count up the extra tiles and check my score sheet. My worst fears are confirmed. Those extra points put Norman White over the top. He's won again. Dave proudly announces that the champion has retained the ABSP UK Open.

I slump down in my chair. Of course, it was unlikely that anyone would dethrone such a wonderful player, but it was so close. It's like losing a five thousand pound bet, just like the 73' Open final — the one that got away. Mikkael rises from his chair and shakes the champion's hand. 'What a splendid game, Mr Norman.' A yawn takes hold, and I cast my mind forward to a good night's sleep and waking to the Telegraph crossword.

A few well-wishers approach the champion and the journalist waits patiently with her dictaphone. Mikkael's name will not be in tomorrow's headline but the community will be talking about this match for years to come. Nearly three hundred points for one word. The tournament players and other spectators gather round, wanting to give him a pat on the back. He cuts a different figure from the lonely foreigner fixated on his old computer the day before. Perhaps there's hope for me, too. He takes out the yellow camera and gets a few group shots to remember the moment.

It's a full five minutes before I can offer my commiserations. 'Tough break, kiddo,' I say, giving Mikkael a sympathetic tap.

He's still wired from the adrenaline of the game. 'Ha haa. Yes, it was a very proximate game, no?'

Mona clamps herself to his arm and can't resist chipping in. 'So unlucky! You look like you need a drink.' She offers him her lemonade and Mikkael gulps it down in one. Mona feigns surprise that he's just stolen her entire drink. He seems revived. 'I thought I'd be able to say I lost to the champ,' she says. 'But I'm still proud of you. You nearly did it.' She goes up on tiptoes and plants a kiss on his cheek. For once, Mikkael doesn't laugh.

I offer him a warm handshake, gripping his elbow with my free hand. 'You know, that's the biggest word score we've ever had in the tournament, and you still get the £1,000 runners-up prize.'

He grins his snaggletoothed smile.

'The award ceremony will be on stage in about ten minutes.' I slip him an ABSP business card, and tell him to contact me if he needs anything, Scrabble related or otherwise.

'Yes, Mr Warren,' he says. 'I would like to send you my computer application for a 3D Scrabble to participate online.'

'I'm not sure my old desktop computer knows how to handle 3D games.'

Mikkael unzips his bag and thrusts his laptop into my hands. 'Please, it would be honorary to stay in touch. It is loaded on here. Now we can play together online.'

Surely he needs to keep his laptop for work, to support his family.

'I buy new one tomorrow with my prize money,' he says. 'Please.'

I don't know if it is the high emotion of the day, the late hour, or the fact he and Mona remind me so much of my early days in the Scrabble community, but a lump builds in my throat. 'Thank you, young man. It will be *honorary* to play you online.'

It's not often I meet new people. Most of my friends are six feet under. I'll enjoy exchanging news with him via email. Perhaps 3D Scrabble will become a part of the ABSP events one day. Anyway, it's nice to know he's found a like-minded soul in Mona. I'm not sure about those tattoos, but she's a kind girl. For a second I imagine them married, at home, with verbacious little tracksuited children sitting on the carpet in front of them. Perhaps they'll go to Guatemala on honeymoon, look for quetzals, and reminisce about the tournament that brought them together.

'You must be hungry,' I say to Mikkael. 'I can give you a lift to Coventry's finest kebab establishment on the way home.'

Before long, we're sharing a meal, crammed into the small seating area of Eastern Treats. We search for the most valuable item on the dimly lit menu display.

Donner, kofte, falafel. Then I see it. 'Shawarma,' I say. 'Nineteen points.'

Ludgate Circus Crossing

Tiny people on the street below scurry across the road. You watch. It's good looking down from twelve storeys up. The only person you know on a higher floor is a management consultant — a career choice so feckless that you considered becoming one just so you could advise your colleagues to get a more useful job. Perhaps that's why there aren't many skyscrapers in The City of London. They'd just fill them with more management consultants.

The people on the crossing fizz across the street like loose electrons bonded only to their phones. Two of them bump into each other but there's no reaction. You're fed up with *your* phone. Most of the notifications display your boss's inane questions or pictures of your friends' ugly babies. You still haven't replied to Jemima's dinner party invitation because you have no one to bring. Was there ever a moment when we had the perfect balance between life and gadgets? Sometime in the nineties, you think. Beepers, that was it. Useful, but not too intrusive. You make a vague plan to start a Mennonite-like sect which caps technology at a 1994 level.

The intersection is a four-way crossing like they have in Japan. Frowning lawyers and investment bankers juggle coffees and copies of City AM, all seemingly one ball short of a full set. A young upstart crosses on an electric unicycle. The Council can't decide if they should go on the pavement, the cycle lane or straight to the bottom of the bloody Thames. In spite of the chaos, you love the crossing. You spend a good portion of your day watching the action.

After this morning's rubbernecking, you'll be late with the financial projections you're preparing for Scotch-Bright Sponges. Maybe you could stay late. *Sorry, Jemima.* But your boss would roll his eyes and use this as another excuse to keep you on the tiddling accounts at the foot of the bill. He didn't even acknowledge your joke about doing a 'clean job'.

Without a decent bonus this year, your life plan will come tumbling down. You've got five years tops before your Tinder account stops getting any right swipes and your bosoms morph into curtain folds of flab. By that time, even Pervy Pete in the local off-licence will have stopped asking you out. Take action now. Set something up.

Outside you see a painted face among the crowd. The Clown. You hate that guy. Why can't he get a real job like the rest of the country? Perhaps he's French. They have whole colleges devoted to clowning over there. You wonder if he lives in a squat in New Cross and cooks dinners for a ragtag bunch of activists and penniless photographers. Look at him, prancing around with his lame routine. And the costume! Curly hair bulging out of the swimming cap, white gloves and a stripy t-shirt. What a joke.

You've had 'coulrophobia' ever since a clown threw a bucket of glitter over you at Jenny Bartlett's seventh birthday party. You had an asthma attack, then you had a panic attack. It was so upsetting that you forgot to take home your party bag and missed out on a miniature My Little Pony and some top-notch cake. You were coughing up sparkles for days. How can anyone like clowns? They're devious. At least the ones at the rodeo get a few kicks from the bulls.

An alert pops up on screen. Barnaby is on the move. The cat-cam seemed like a fantastic idea at the time, but it's become a time-stealing bandit. It did help you discover why the spider plant in the lounge is dying a slow death. You watch him stretch his furry legs, march around in a circle, spray the poor plant, and flop onto the rug as if he's been shot with a tranquiliser dart. A job well done. You make a note in your online calendar to move the plant to the balcony. Another entry informs you that there is a Dawson's Creek marathon on E4 tonight and that the jam roly-poly in the fridge will be out of date soon. Surely you can organise something better for a Friday night.

Down below, Antoine (you've given him that name even though you've never met him) is pissing people off as usual. Last week you saw a woman smack him with her handbag. It made your day. His act consists of jumping in front of people, pretending there's an invisible wall between them, then thrusting his hand out for spare change. He only gets a few seconds before the lights change and the stampede begins.

You sometimes think about keeping statistics on the crossing. For example, the number of times people fall over (none so far today), the percentage of men wearing pink shirts, or the estimated hourly income of Antoine. He probably earns more than you, the bastard. It's already eleven twenty-five and the report document is still sitting open on your screen, waiting for the show to start. Maybe you could write a light-hearted article about life in The City of London accompanied by the crossing stats. One of the free papers might publish it. You might even get a date out of it.

It clouds over and you sense a shitstorm coming. There won't be any play in the test match, and without cricket, the partners will have nothing to talk about. They'll go round the office and flirt with all the women under thirty, which of course excludes you. You may as well be fifty in their eyes.

Coldplay groans out over the radio in their depressingly successful way, and the wall of windows separating the office tower from the street turns grey. Workers around you pull on cardigans and suit jackets, even though the dry office air remains at a strict constant of nineteen degrees. You find yourself looking out the window again.

The rain performs a drum roll on the roof and lightning flickers in the distance behind St Paul's Cathedral. At the crossing, Antoine sits in the middle of the road. What's that silly French bugger doing now? You press your face to the cold glass window to get a better look. There's no traffic, and all the pedestrians have scarpered. His white makeup runs down his face, and the rain has now slicked his bushy hair. He must be freezing.

Can Antoine see you staring from all the way down there? Yes, he's definitely looking. Then he points! He mouths your name, then, lifting his hands in front of him, he does his little glass wall routine, miming the invisible barrier.

You reach out and touch the window in front of you. 'Me?' It seems a stretch, but you are willing to believe anything to avoid crying to Dawson's Creek.

Still cross-legged, Antoine rises up and hovers above the ground like a levitating Buddhist monk. This is too much. Your mind thunders. Why doesn't he do *this* trick for the punters? It looks so real and not a single person is there to see it. You fumble for your phone to record him, but you drop it in the kerfuffle. The screen's cracked. Bugger!

'Quick. Come and look,' you say to the three office drones nearby.

Bald Barry glares at you as though you're a cockroach in his sandwich, then goes back to his screen.

When you look out the window again, Antoine has floated higher. He must be two meters above the ground. How is he pulling this one off? It's better than his mime routine, that's for sure. The tapping of computer keys and the drone of Chris Martin continue in the background and you begin to accept that it would take more than a rocket-powered clown for anyone to tear their gaze from ever-changing algorithms on their computer screens. No one will believe you without your phone, which is now leaking inky fluid across its screen.

After a few seconds, he raises his arms and blasts up into the air as if he's the steam purging from a pressure cooker. Wet through and with white gloves pointed to the heavens, the clown shoots skyward, increasing in speed. Your mouth hangs agape. Remember to breathe. Antoine flies up, his stripy shirt and red boots getting ever smaller. This is not going to do your coulrophobia any good. You strain your eyes, but Antoine disappears into elephant-grey clouds.

A lightning strike pierces the sky in front of the office. The sound is thunderous and your heart jumps up and down like it's on a trampoline. People finally look up, grumbling in mild surprise, then go back to their typing. You're speechless, not that you could say anything. They'd think you are mad.

After what happened, there's no chance you'll get any work done. That report will get written when pigs— when *clowns* fly. You slump into your ergonomic computer chair and drink a whole bottle of peach flavoured fizzy water in one. *Christ on a bike.*

In the toilets, the buzzing broken strip light above the mirror pings on and off. Your mind wavers between putting the whole incident down to the fact you skipped breakfast, and requesting the number of the nearest psychiatrist with an available appointment. There's no way you can casually drop a gravity-defying circus performer into a conversation. 'Did anyone watch Eastenders last night? No? Well, did anyone see Chuckles the Clown turn himself into Apollo 18 on the crossing?' Even eating the double-chocolate cake bar in your handbag doesn't bring you back to the real world. When you look in the mirror, a pallid woman with flat hair and hollow pupils looks back. You splash water on your face, but it makes your foundation run like Antoine's makeup. The wicked witches in accounts give each other a look when you emerge from the bathroom. *Someone's been crying again.*

The expensive pedometer watch on your wrist beeps 1 PM: only two-thousand steps so far. In the last hour, all you've done is work on your crossing statistics spreadsheet and buy another Halloween costume for Barnaby online. You've scoured the street for signs of Antoine without success. You'd love to speak to him now but the chance has gone. Always the way. He's probably rocketing over the English Channel by now, squirting water onto passing seagulls with his trick flower.

At lunch, you discover that you can access the Tinder App through your computer. No matches. Still, six hours before you have to show up at Jemima's without a date, or skulk home to Barnaby and the dying pot plant. The chicken in your Caesar salad tastes of cardboard; the lettuce is soggy and tastes the same. The croutons might actually be made of cardboard.

Although you *have* to get that report done before lunch is over, you can't resist going down to the crossing to do some detective work. It's still overcast but the rain has stopped. Perhaps Antoine left a scorch mark from his bum-based jet fumes. When you get down to the street, there's no sign of your French friend. You wait at the lights then participate in the scrimmage, charging towards the opposite corner, dodging the groups of tossers with spiky hair and Bluetooth earpieces. Even though you go back and forth several times, you see no trace of clown makeup or modelling balloons. What were you expecting, his business card and a box of coloured handkerchiefs?

'Excuse me,' you say to the kiosk vendor a few meters from the crossing, 'was there a clown here earlier?'

'I see a lot of clowns around these parts, darlin'.' He laughs a toothless cockney laugh.

Everyone's a comedian today. 'No, an *actual* clown, you know, white face, swimming cap, looks terrifying.'

'Like this fella?' He points to a top-shelf magazine covered with tissue paper. A man in a clown mask hovers menacingly behind a naked woman. The title reads *The Naughty Circus*. Brilliant, more nightmares.

Your mind's racing like the little green man on the traffic light when there's only five seconds left to cross. How did he do it? 'Never mind,' you stammer.

The old man laughs as you leave.

As you ride the lift back up to the twelfth floor, you check yourself in the mirror — even worse than before. For a split second, the masked man from the porn mag flashes up behind you with his evil grin.

Your whole body tenses with the shock and your legs give out. Darkness. When you can bring yourself to open your eyes, you scoot around to face him but he's not there. You ride the last few floors hugging your knees, your bum stuck to the carpet.

The doors spring open and the secretary at the front desk peers into the lift, wondering why one of the firm's up-and-coming financial analysts is sat on her arse, having a panic attack. You consider doing a forward roll out of the lift (and possibly finishing with jazz hands) but you doubt that you can pull it off, so you dust yourself down and mumble something about yoga stretches to the secretary on the way back to your work station. Breathing returns to normal.

Something is waiting for you on your desk when you get back. It's a full report folder with the Scotch-Bright logo on it. You check the overview on the first page. It's perfect — Helvetica New, twelve-point, cells aligned right and colour-coded. As you flip through the quarterly figures, you see that everything is exactly as your boss would demand. Just as you ask yourself who could have done this, a Post-it Note flutters out of the file onto the desk. It reads:

When I told my dad I wanted to become a clown, he said I'd have some big shoes to fill.

It must be him. Does he work at your firm and secretly rush down to perform on the street? As long as there is nothing funny about his calculations, you're happy to pass his work off as yours. You scurry towards your boss's office and knock on the frosted glass. Monty Gladstone.

'Step right up.'

What fresh hell does he have in store today? You compose yourself.

'Come on then!' he barks.

When you enter he sits behind his desk, puffing his chest and twizzling his moustache. 'Ladies and Gentlemen, our *brightest* analyst.'

'... Scotch-Bright.' You hand the folder to him, praying he'll look at it later. 'Sorry it's late.'

'Hope you've scoured it for errors?' he says.

That was *your* joke, and he's passing it off as his own. Typical. 'Err, squeaky clean, sir.'

He lets out a roaring laugh. 'Excellent.'

Relief. You turn to leave.

'Wait a moment,' he says. You stop with your hand on the door. What's he seen?

'What do you think of this?' He reaches under his desk and pulls out a black top hat. 'Taking the clients to Ascot tomorrow. Decent or what?' He nests the hat on top of his balding head and twists his moustache again. It's uncanny, he's just missing the red jacket.

'Very handsome, sir,' you reply, then you run for the exit.

Now the ordeal is over, you can focus on the crossing at Ludgate Circus for the rest of the day. It's best not to think about whether you completely invented a flying clown and subconsciously wrote the report. You read about workplace schizophrenia once. It seems quite inconvenient. Your phone bleeps. The screen is still damaged, so you can't see the entire message. It's a Tinder match. You rush to log in on your computer screen.

Jacques, 38, London: *Girls say they want a guy who is funny and spontaneous, but when I tap on the window at night dressed as a clown it's all screaming.*

The picture that accompanies the message looks vaguely like Antoine without his makeup. You decide to play along: *It'll take more than one joke for me to get over my fear of clowns.*

He asks if you know what they say about guys with big shoes.

Big Feet?

Jacques replies. *I've been scouring the app for months for a bright one like you.*

So the report *was* him. Today has been so confusing you feel like you've bet your sanity on a game of three-card shuffle. You sit and stare at the screen. A minute passes.

Jacques: Are you still there?

You check another text, in which Jemima says she's invited an eligible friend. Unbelievable. Like buses, apart from the fact that one of the buses is probably an actuary who wears gilets and once climbed Snowden, and the other one can fly.

There's no competition. You reply to Jacques and leave Jemima unread. *How do I know you're for real?*

Jacques: Tricks are no fun unless they're in person.

Your texting wit has deserted you. Today has been exhausting. Are you going to go on a date with a street performer who has a working knowledge of financial reporting software, access to your office space and the ability to levitate?

Jacques:... 6 pm at the crossing?

He might have tickets to *Cirque du Soleil* at the Royal Albert Hall, but then again he might drag you into the sewers of New Cross, murder you and serve you up to his squatmates. Then you see it. On closer inspection, the pink of his collar peeks into his profile photo. Be honest, you've always admired men who are in touch with their feminine side. This one wears makeup too. Your fingers start tapping.

You: I suppose you won't reveal the secret of how you pulled it off...

Jacques waits for a bit, then sends three emojis — a rocket, a clown face and an aubergine followed by a question mark.

You smirk. If a guy can't impress a girl by obtaining a superpower and doing a spotless job on a quarterly report, then what is it going to take?

You: All systems go.

Six o'clock is only a few hours away. Let the planning commence. You set your DVR to remote record Dawson's Creek and promise yourself you won't demolish the jam roly-poly when you come in drunk at midnight. The rows and columns of the crossing statistics present themselves in a perfect strongman tower formation. Your finger hovers over the Recycle Bin icon. *Are you sure?* You hit delete.

Satellite of Love

Lift Off

We blasted off that night on our joint mission, up through layers of decreasing resistance, through rarified air, away from the turbulence of our lives, and at that time, we burned white-hot as the payload jettisoned and we drifted into the blissful tranquility of space, staring back in wonder, two satellites guided by each other's blips and bleeps.

Orbit

As we travelled around and around, the years passing, we fell into a pattern of signals and silences, with burning desire transformed into morning briefings, precision operations, and the occasional recorrective thrust, and like this we circled, pretending that our steady progress was just as exciting as the initial countdown, and in our orbit, we looked down at others, wondering if they could reach us without help, but whereas I stepped in with wayfinding pointers, you found flaws and imperfections, and the beauty we saw diverged, with me drawn back towards to the launch site, and you slowly drifting off-line, our bond loosening as every day you asked me to reach further into the darkness, to bridge a gap that neither of us could compute.

Lost Signal

When I crashed back to Earth, I thought I heard your voice still guiding me away from catastrophic failure, directing left or right, with me merging into the flow, then exiting, folding back on myself like a twisted used up tin can, recalculating past behaviours, praying for those words 'you have reached your destination', and finally arriving there, my scorched feet crunching the driveway shingle only to find that my destination was no longer a home because you had left years ago, and as your velocity sped you far away, into eternity, your voice weakened and cut out, before silence washed over... and I learned to navigate on my own.

Happysad

Dying was the easy part. When my children moved to Amsterdam, and later, when my husband departed this world, I endured difficult times. But hardest of all was the day I accepted the only way to escape my agony was to leave my body behind.

With each passing year, I lost friends and family to illness, and the dull aches in my joints became louder. By the time I was seventy, I could no longer walk. I couldn't eat with a knife and fork, and while some people were worse off — paralysed, or with brains lost to dementia — that was no comfort.

That difficult day came at Utrecht General Hospital. The doctor informed me my bones were too brittle for replacements, more chemical painkillers the only option. My daughters Sanne and Lara stood either side of the bed, hanging on the doctor's every word.

'What about marijuana?' I asked. 'Some people at the residence use it.'

My daughters suddenly stood to attention. It can't have been easy hearing their mother asking for the drugs they warned their children about.

The doctor replied without looking up from his notes. 'Some patients find it useful, but for marijuana

215

prescriptions, we are required to provide proof that the opioid medications have been ineffective.'

I found them ineffective. They numbed my body and made me feel sick. Wasn't that proof enough? I lived my life from pill to pill in constant search of equilibrium. They stole my appetite, so I came to resemble a broomstick with wiry hair. My bruised pincushion hands hung by my sides.

'That stuff will make you cloudy-headed, mother,' said Lara.

I knew the effects. I was young once. Light up a joint and it gives you that warm, safe feeling, but when it wears off you feel like you've forgotten something. My Edward used to call it a cocktail of happy and sad. Even if it provided a brief respite from the pain, I resolved to source some cannabis.

'This can't go on, doctor,' I said. Then, I got tearful. My body crumbling so early was cruel. It was the first time in a long time I'd cried. Lara put her hand on mine before remembering that it caused me discomfort. She passed a tissue and I dabbed my eyes. I drew breath and asked the question to cast it out of my mind. 'And what about assisted suicide? Is that possible in my situation?'

'Mother! How could you say such—'

I cut her off by raising my hand. Sanne gave me the same stare abuse victims use for the accused on the dock. That hurt me more than the arthritis.

The doctor told me that they made assessments. I'd need appointments with a counsellor. A long process.

We drove back to the residence in difficult silence. We were together, but from then on I'd also be alone, against them. My girls would go for coffee and formulate a plan to keep me dependent on the prescriptions and appointments. I didn't blame them but it broke something between us. From that point, death was the beginning of a pain-free existence, not the end of a painful life.

After eighteen months in the retirement community, I had friends. William and Mary were a lovely couple, older than me, and in better health. Then I watched them go. The fourth player in our card group, Stijn, went to hospital with a faulty aorta.

We had our own rooms and access to a modern cafeteria. The communal lounges filled with residents talking over the babble of the TV. The card group sometimes played with the four students granted free accommodation in exchange for their help with the day-to-day running of the place. But time whittled my bones. It pained me that I could no longer walk in the gardens, or turn the pages of a book without help. Increasingly, I wished for the peace that death would bring, just as one pines for home after a long journey.

The Tuesday after the hospital visit, my grandson Kees visited after his music classes. The boy had a spirited soul. Sanne complained about his bad university grades and social *faux pas*, but the boy would go far in life. He had the same long-haired charm as my Edward.

'*Grootmoeder* Anniek. *Grootmoeder* Anniek,' he said, dancing on approach.

'Hello, my boy. How were your classes?'

'Eesh. Tons of reading.'

It would be a good qualification, even if he did want to be a DJ. I listened to his latest electronic composition through his big headphones. It was too intricate and fast for my understanding, beats firing like lasers.

The registered nurse arrived to give me my daily injections. Kees winced as she struggled to find blood vessels. 'Does it hurt, *grootje*?'

It hurt whether I had them or not. Pain is a constant when you have arthritis. 'Have you ever ground your teeth by accident?' I asked. 'That's what my bones feel like.'

We sat there while the nurse continued. She massaged the solution into my fingers and wrist, then moved on to my right hand. Then she moved on to another patient.

'Kees. Could you bring me some marijuana next time you come? They won't give me a prescription.'

He didn't laugh. He took me seriously. 'Does the medication not work?'

I'd tried medication. I'd tried meditation, controlled breathing, imaginary writing, group therapy, electrolysis, pills and injections. 'Nothing frees me completely, so I'd like to try.'

Before he left, my grandson promised to buy me some marijuana sweets — edibles he called them. I never much liked smoking.

As a precaution, I asked Nasser, one of the student residents to sit with me while I swallowed the strawberry-flavoured gummies. I didn't want to end up slumped in the corner. For a long time, nothing happened. We just looked at each other. It took more than half an hour before a Caribbean warm glaze washed over me. My skin tingled as if sprinkled with salt water droplets drying in the sun.

'How are you feeling, Anniek? Do you need a cold drink?'

'No, my darling.' I listened and stared while my thoughts came slowly into focus. I considered my achievements and failures, my loves and losses, my children, and my favourite drug-dealer grandson. My pain morphed from a nagging ache to a dull glow. I asked Nasser something that had been rattling around my mind for some time. 'What do you believe happens…'

Nasser straightened to attention, readying himself for the question.

I finished my thought. '… when you die?'

He thought awhile. 'We believe that *Malak al-Maut* appears to the dying in order to take their souls.'

I admired that about Muslims. They had an unwavering belief in their righteous path home. I looked around the room, concerned about eavesdroppers. 'What about the sinners?'

It seemed like an eternity before he replied. When he did, he spoke as if quoting from the scriptures. 'Sinners' souls are extracted in a most excruciating way, while the honourable are treated kindly.'

I didn't ask what percentage of people deserved a dignified death. Most of the residents who had died in my time at the retirement community had faded away to nothing, their friends and family absent in their last days. I saw no dignity or honour.

The effects of the gummy sweet distorted my world into a time-lapse video with each moment appearing in high definition. I watched the other residents shuffle to and fro in the lounge. Each move in checkers took hours, but the game flew by. The lottery numbers appeared on the television but were gone before anyone noticed them. Staff clattered endlessly in the kitchen. Nasser studied his book.

After watching this scene unfold, I told Nasser I'd like to die.

He wasn't as shocked as my daughters. 'You mean assisted suicide? We studied this for our human rights class.'

'Oh yes?'

He clasped his hands in a scholarly way. 'Almost five per cent of all deaths in The Netherlands are euthanasia.'

'The doctor told me it was reserved for the hopeless.'

'And do you feel hopeless?'

'My only hope is that I'm heading towards another life, embracing it. It will bring peace.'

He was quiet for a full minute. Muslims don't believe in euthanasia. He said he was sure I had considered all of my options, my family too.

In a way, Nasser was right. I considered what I would do and where I might go in the afterlife. However it turned out, it was a better option than my illness grinding me to dust. I thanked him for listening and he returned to his study.

As the effects of the drug lessened, my nerves prickled into focus. Perception of the present moment sharpened. The whole feeling swelled and ebbed; it was bittersweet. Only dying could bring me the feeling of wholeness I desired. I could live pain-free and watch over everyone whom I loved. The infinity of death stored memories, and I wished to reconnect with them. The residents had retired to their rooms. Nasser sat close, still reading his book on law.

In the months that followed, I started the process of seeking my own death. The doctor signed my forms, and they passed the review panel. My condition worsened. Bedbound, with little interest in food. The looks of concern from the nurses changed to those of resignation.

Kees came to visit each week and played me his digital music. I told him I didn't want any more of his candies. Then I asked him to do one thing for his grandma — take down a letter to my daughters. He agreed and I began to dictate.

Sanne, Lara, grandchildren, this is my suicide note.
We will say a final goodbye before I go. The date is
set one week from now. I am so grateful for the love

and times you provided, but the only way to process all that I have lived is to release myself from pain.
I hope I have been a good person and that my journey to the next life will be an easy one. Although we cannot stay together, I will be glad to leave my body behind. It is no longer fit for this world.
Live your best lives.
Your loving mother.

Seeing that boy's hand shake as he wrote was another moment of happysad. It would be his last visit, and we were fiercely proud of each other.

The day I died was one of my better days. My girls arrived with lillies, which brought the scent of summer into the hospital room. I wore my own clothes, not a hospital gown. The doctor connected me to the barbiturate and would administer the lethal dose once I went under.

We looked through a photo album that Lara had compiled. Faded colours, family holidays in France, birthdays, anniversaries, Edward's long hair, the girls' graduations, newborn baby Kees. Sanne read a letter from her two children. She didn't get halfway through before breaking down.

'Girls,' I said, 'I am travelling towards these memories, not away from them.'

Though they drew close, the souls of their eyes had retreated. There was nothing left to say. I had no more tears. It must have seemed callous, but I'd cried them all out. The thought of boosting the euthanasia numbers by one pleased me. *Five per cent of deaths*, I'll always remember that.

Sanne and Lara held one pincushion hand while I gripped the medication trigger in the other. The doctor watched from the corner of the room, his clipboard cradled like a baby.

'I'm going towards peace,' I said, and with one last agonising squeeze of my right hand, I depressed the dosage button.

As I departed my body, the illusion lifted. The physical simulation of a life is only one millionth of true freedom. After death, your history, your actions and the purpose of all the events in your life becomes clear — they build experience for your soul to live in its real home. Releasing myself from the chronic pain of life was my greatest achievement.

In the afterlife, you may interact with any person or event with which you've had contact. I've spoken with the 6,231 other souls who committed legal suicide that year. I've visited the coast of France again and felt the breeze on my skin. I move freely and without pain.

The afterlife is everything and nothing. Exactly what I am now is unknown. Perhaps I'm trapped in the exact moment of my physical death, and in that millisecond, I experience my personal eternity. The veil of time lifts. I will visit every place I've known, thousands of years into the past and into the future. I'll visit loved ones at any point in their lives as if they're here with me. Reality becomes malleable. I can replay and edit any conversation, sound or sensation from my seventy-five years on the planet.

It pleases me to know I lived a good life, at least according to Nasser's principles. Along the way, I discovered that life in your physical body is just a fact-finding mission, a collection of sensory data. I went along accumulating it all, filling my afterlife with precious possessions for me to enjoy forever. My loves, my failures, my accomplishments, my pain. Every emotion I experienced, every lesson learned now blends into empathy and understanding. Perhaps that's what happysad really is.

The afterlife is waiting for my children, my grandchildren, those in the residence and all who will pass. It is waiting for you and it is beautiful.

Hello, you

Revenge is all about the minor details. If I moved things around too much, she'd notice. As well as having elephant-like ankles, she had a memory like one too. So, I nudged things an inch to the left one day, then two to the right the next, playing the slow game. Eventually, she would crack. This haunting was my payback.

I'd gone to such efforts to please her when I was alive — cooking insipid recipes to the letter, following the instructions on her cleaning spreadsheet, and settling for the title of fourth most important man in her life (behind her sixty-year-old lover and her two poodles). While I preferred Douglas Adams books and gardening, Alison enjoyed combing the knots out of their fur, and stroking another man's 'best friend'.

Most of my headaches came from Alison's daily allegations or those yapping poodles, so it was a surprise to me when I met my maker at just fifty. I'd been in good health, then suddenly, *bam*, a brain aneurysm.

Back in the kitchen, Alison cocked her head as she reached for her slim-shake sachets. *What kind of game was this?* She rearranged them, scolding the packets as if they were unruly schoolchildren. Just wait until she finds the batteries missing out of the Dustbuster. She drank her high-performance drink and fed Benjamin and Gerrald their one scoop of biscuits each. Another element of my little rebellion was to switch up the food in the packets so that Gerry, the portly one, kept piling on the pounds, while his brother ate the high-fibre pellets. The growing differential between her dogs baffled Alison. She must have thought that Gerry was also sneaking doughnuts on the way to work.

After the dogs had finished and their bowls had been inspected, wiped clean, disinfected then stacked in their designated place, Alison wrote a to-do list for *him*, and went out for her morning power walk. I suspected she just walked to the bakery and back. I wished I could have followed her, but I was destined to stay behind and complete my mission.

It's true I never loved the dogs, but I was mortified when they were poisoned. I'm no murderer. The silly pair got into a packet of my slug pellets that must've looked like their kibble. And they say curiosity killed the cat. Her pets eventually recovered, but Alison didn't. She could have just divorced me, but she wouldn't let sleeping dogs lie.

As I waited at the kitchen table, I decided that today would be the day. I needed to push the action and elicit the reaction I'd been tasked with. Otherwise I'd end up just as depressed as when I'd been married to her. Besides, *he* was around, so my little game would have another unsuspecting victim.

He was Brian, a Brigadier in the British Army, with ruddy cheeks and a public-school voice. Alison always hated my ponytail, so I'm not surprised she went for a 'short back and sides' type. Even though they had married, they didn't see each other often enough for his domestic misdemeanours to bother Alison too much. I think they actually preferred synchronising schedules to living together in domestic bliss. When I started my haunting a couple of years ago, I wondered where Brian would fit into the pecking order, but he soon had the dogs well-drilled.

They were the perfect fit. Alison valued cleanliness and order, and Brian liked classical music and tin soldiers. I'm not kidding. He was even more serious about his battlefield arrangements than Alison was with her coordinated cushion displays. They met at the Arms Expo, although this did not translate to fireworks in the bedroom.

The dogs lay in their beds and I twiddled my thumbs in the kitchen. I've had plenty of time to do this since the moment after my death — my transformation from *patsy* to poltergeist. When I woke, white walls surrounded me, and it wasn't Saint Peter I heard, but a computerised voice.

'Appearance, communication, or movement?' it asked in a soft American accent.

I looked around, but all I could see was blinding white. 'Where on Earth am I?'

'You are not on Earth. In fact, you do not exist in any physical form, you are—'

'Wait. I know that voice. Stephen Hawking?'

'The Intel ACAT system has been selected as the most appropriate voice to represent your creator,' it replied. I suppose I did always admire the man. His wife supposedly bullied him too.

'Homicide victim eight-one-nine, you must now choose appearance, communication or movement.'

'Homicide?'

The voice sighed.

I was surprised Dr Hawking needed a programmed sigh, but then again he was always a bit of a sarcastic type.

'You were murdered and have therefore been retained to haunt your killer until atonement is achieved.'

I knew things had been going badly between us, but murder?

'Your wife added concentrated slug poison into your food, drinks, and cosmetic products. You had a stroke.'

Talk about a toxic relationship. 'She really must have thought I wanted the dogs dead…'

'You must now return to the scene of the crime, to haunt her conscience as a poltergeist, through selected visions, by communication through a medium, or via the movement of objects. You may choose only one.'

'Won't she be going to prison?' I asked.

Another robot sigh escaped. 'A brain tumour was discovered during your autopsy, and what with your advancing age, the police didn't—'

'Alright, Stephen, don't rub it in! I know I was getting on, but... that slimy woman.' The snails were going to have a field day in the garden now.

After careful consideration, I chose the power of movement. I certainly had nothing to say to Alison, and had always maintained that spirit mediums were a hoax. What The Great Stephen didn't tell me, was that I'd have to stay around the house until Alison was sorry for her crimes. She never seemed to feel guilty about anything, but I wasn't just going to spell it out to Alison and move on. I wanted to exact the perfect revenge, taking my time to send her over the edge. Now, after two years with little success, it felt like I was only punishing myself.

Last week, The Brigadier returned from his posting in Cyprus. I'd waged a prolonged campaign of gaslighting against his wife and the cracks were starting to show. Now he stood at the door in his immaculate khaki uniform. During his two weeks of leave I would turn up the heat to boiling point.

'Hello, you,' she said. 'I'm so glad you're here, darling.'

He dropped his holdall and saluted. He actually saluted. 'Brigadier Jevons reporting for duty.' In truth, he looked more like a sandbag with a moustache than a Brigadier.

Ben and Gerry stood guard beside Alison, sniffing the bag before falling in line. He patted them on the head. 'Benjamin. Gerald.'

It was sickening to watch my murderous ex-wife and my direct replacement (better with a bayonet, worse with a trowel) play house. This had to end soon.

'Shall we get a brew on?' he asked, looking at his watch.

'Yes, darling. You get yourself unpacked.'

He went upstairs with his kit bag and the dogs followed at a respectful distance.

Over the next couple of days, I watched their holiday patterns develop. The Brigadier completed his exercise routine at 0600 hours sharp (his wife didn't join in), showered (again without Alison), and pulled on a fresh polo shirt and slacks, before presenting himself for inspection. He looked like a walking advertisement for *Off-Duty Officer* magazine. After breakfast, he set up his model soldiers in the conservatory and stayed away from Drill Sergeant Alison for the remainder of the morning. I assume she made her secret visits to the bakery during the early dog walk.

During their time off, I was hard at work shifting things around, making ever more obvious movements of Alison's trinkets, and playing fast and loose with The Brigadier's belongings.

'Have you seen the Dijon, love?' she barked.

In the conservatory, the man fiddled with his soldiers. 'Mustard? No. Can't stand the stuff.'

Off she went to the shops, and I returned the two missing jars to the shelf. *Stick that in your ham sandwich.*

Every time Brian went to the toilet, I made sure to lift the seat back up and splash a small puddle on the floor. I left lights on all over the house, ironed the creases out of his slacks, took in the waists on Alison's trousers, and shortened the dogs' leads by one inch per day.

The tension increased, and over the course of one week, they went from cuddles on the sofa, to sleeping in separate beds. Some holiday. While Alison researched new cleaning products and watched reruns of Midsomer Murders, he spent more and more time with his spectacles perched on his nose, observing the various maps of historical battles spread out on the table.

Moving The Brigadier's tin soldiers around was the most fun I'd had in years. I'd quite forgotten that I was supposed to be concentrating on Alison. He was so careful where he placed the miniature guns, horses and flags, attaining military precision with the use of a magnifying glass.

Alison returned from her power walk, and I got ready to ramp up the action. That morning, I really stuck it to Brian's troops, switching armaments, toppling soldiers left and right, and even removing all of the brigadiers from the scene. Each time he came back to his battle, he was ever more exasperated.

'Alison, darling? Have the dogs been in here?'

She paused her 'search and destroy' mission of the microscopic honey droplets I'd left on the floor. 'Don't be silly. Gerald's with me, and Benjamin's in the garden. Look.'

'Hmm. They *must have* been nosing around where they don't belong.'

Alison pointed a finger. 'And I suppose it was *them* who left the toilet seat up again.'

The Brigadier did not like *that* accusation. He was used to giving orders, not receiving them. 'Nonsense. I always leave the lavvy as I find it. And please don't touch my pieces.'

Alison mumbled that his piece wasn't in any danger of being touched, and went back to her cleaning. The Brigadier performed an inspection of the latrines to rid himself of the charge of leaving the seat up. While he was gone, I quickly rearranged The Battle of Waterloo to make it look as though the French had won and Napoleón was buggering The Duke of Wellington.

When he returned, his face went redder than the British uniforms. 'This is not a game, woman!'

Alison marched into the conservatory. 'What is it now, Brian? Honestly, you and your bloody toy soldiers.'

The Brigadier picked up the nearest piece to hand — a lead field gun about the size of a King Edward potato. 'Stay out of here!' he commanded, launching his projectile.

He didn't mean to hit her, of that I'm sure, but the toy gun clonked Alison right on the head. She stumbled backwards, crashing into the kitchen like a concussed rhinoceros, knocking over the dogs' food in the process. Kibble everywhere. I watched in amazement as she struggled for footing and slipped on the wet floor. Her head slammed on the edge of the freshly-wiped kitchen counter and she went down.

Alison held her temple, groaning. She rolled under the table, leaving a viscous trail of blood on the lino. She stared up at the underside of the table and probably wondered why someone had stencilled the logo for *Slug Away* onto the wood. (I'd planned to put these messages all around the house, but at least she got to see it once before she went). Her head spasmed and her hands clawed at the air. Even if they found a brain tumour when they performed *her* autopsy, it wouldn't explain the hole in her head caused by the fall.

The Brigadier was beside himself. He even left The Duke of Wellington to the mercy of Bonaparte and rushed in to administer CPR. The dogs barked and ran in circles, before hoovering up the biscuits on the bloody floor.

Alison was dead in minutes. If that wasn't justice then I didn't know what was. I couldn't have hoped for a better result. I even did a little jig on top of the kitchen table.

The Brigadier phoned the police and turned himself in. Although he hadn't meant to hit her, he would go to jail for manslaughter or worse. It wasn't as if the dogs could exonerate him. Brian wouldn't be able to play with his tin soldiers in prison, but at least he'd be used to the strict routine.

With my mission complete, I was released from my purgatory prison. Relief. I floated through the roof, up into the sky, all the way to the white emptiness of Stephen Hawking's waiting room. Now I could rest in peace.

'Haunting unsuccessful,' said the voice.

I reeled. 'What do you mean unsuccessful? She got exactly what she deserved.'

Stephen sighed. 'She did not atone for her crime.'

My shoulders drew into a high shrug. 'I'm happy with the outcome.'

There was a long pause like he was calculating something. 'Manslaughter victim three-four-nine will now haunt the agent of *her* misjustice.'

'Hold on a minute,' I said.

'And she has elected to appear through selected visions, until justice is served.'

No. It couldn't be. The bright surroundings forced me to screw my eyes shut. My temple pounded.

When I opened my eyes, a plump, perfectly turned-out events planner stood before me. She wore a pressed suit and a name badge that said Alison Baker. She had a diet milkshake drink in one hand and a miniature metal cannon in the other. As she looked up, she raised a hand to greet me. Although she didn't speak, her words were crystal clear. 'Hello, you.'

Time and Time Again

Click.

Something bad always happens when you touch red buttons.

Mr. Smiggles lifts his furry head and looks at me with yellow eyes. I must look funny wearing the helmet. Well, I can press the button if I want; it's *my* Robotix G50 helmet, not his. What does Mr. Smiggles know anyway? He's only seven and I'm nearly nine, and sometimes he licks his own bum.

The colours around me go all swirly. The room starts to move and my legs feel funny. I smell something like tuna sandwiches (which I *hate*). Where are we going?

The button is a special feature. I've checked the box, and it's not on any of the pictures. I tried not to press it. At first, I thought about asking my parents, but Daddy says that Mummy pushes his buttons enough, so I decided not to bother them. Now I wish I had an adult to help and not a cat.

The plastic helmet is hot inside and makes your voice sound like Robotix (from the Animatronix series). Robotix is fantastically clever. In every episode, she saves the galaxy by knowing something that seems simple, like tying your shoelaces, but is actually quite difficult… like tying your shoelaces.

We're flying through time and everything whizzes past — dates, newspaper headlines, and the carrots from yesterday's dinner that I hid in my pocket. Robotix never knows where she'll travel, but she always goes somewhere exciting. We'll probably end up in some boring place like Dad's dental practice in Wolverhampton or in the queue at Lloyds Bank.

I've wanted to press that button since I discovered it a week ago. Some buttons aren't supposed to be pressed because they might tape over Top Gear, or delete Mummy's Solitaire statistics, so I waited until after Shrove Tuesday to make sure I didn't get into trouble and miss out on pancakes. It's been hard to keep it a secret from my sister, Greta. She calls me 'Slo-Mo' ever since she got the T1200 for her birthday. Even if it's more advanced, I haven't seen a secret button on *her* helmet.

We land with a bump. Mr. Smiggles jumps out of my hands onto a wooden floor and skids around like he's wearing tiny roller skates. When I take off the helmet, I see decorated tables, a huge buffet, and a hairy man (who looks a bit like a mole in a bomber jacket) setting up a DJ booth. 'Quick,' I say, holding up the tablecloth. 'Under here.' We dive under the long table before the mole man can see us.

'I can't believe that thing actually works,' says Mr. Smiggles. His voice is posher than expected. *Did my cat talk to me?* I pinch Mr. Smiggles to make sure I'm not dreaming. He hisses. 'Infernal child. You pinch *yourself* to check if you are dreaming.'

'Oh, right.' I pinch myself a bit half-heartedly. *Not dreaming*. 'Sorry.'

Even though he can talk, he stays on all fours. He rubs his head against the table leg, scratching an itch.

I know how he feels. I've got eczema on my hands and stupid Greta says I need to be put into quarantine. 'How can you—?'

'Communicate, expostulate, converse, discourse, pronounce and utter?' His voice sounds like Dumbledore from Harry Potter. 'You may finally be able to understand me, but I remain an illiterate feline.'

I've been able to read for at least two years.

He raises a paw like he's going to write something on the whiteboard. 'But, reading is not a valuable life skill, Maureen. Cats need to be agile, not slovenly bookworms.' Smiggles couldn't even catch that mouse in the kitchen. Greta's cat, Donkey-Kong, trapped it, then Daddy put it in the bin. He sticks his tail in the air and marches around. 'Now, child, as you constantly remind me, you are both older and wiser than I, so the floor is yours. I suppose you have some kind of plan'.

A plan… 'We can make a plan while we eat some sandwiches.' I pop up from under the table and see hundreds of neat sandwiches on trays. They're triangular, so you know they're the ones with expensive fillings. Mr. Smiggles will want crab paste, but I like cheese and onion. The table stretches all the way down the side of the tent. It's a big white tent, with pretty decorations hanging from the ceiling. There's a square dance floor and speakers that look even older than the mole man DJ.

'Would you be so kind as to bring me a tuna sandwich, dear?' says Smiggles from under the table. 'And don't upset the display.'

I find a tuna one and take out the cucumber. *Where are we?* The circular tables have flowers in the middle and name tags for each of the places. Mummy and Daddy's names are next to each other on the nicest table. Mr. Smiggles has finished his tuna, and pokes his head out from under the table. He asks what year Roy and Daphne tied the knot.

'What knot?'

He sighs. 'Must I teach you everything, Maureen?' He might think he is cleverer than me, but he chased Greta's laser pen for half an hour before he found out it wasn't real. 'To tie the knot means to get married. We're at your parents' wedding.'

So we're here, but I haven't been born. *Weird.*

The sound of voices comes from outside the tent window. About fifty people (mostly old) are clinking glasses and taking photos on the grass. I try to work out what the year is by counting my fingers. How old is Greta? I'm running out of fingers. Now I'll have to start again. Do thumbs count too? Can I use my toes? It's useless. The people begin to line up at the door.

'Come on, child. It's 1999. They were married five years before Greta's appearance.'

That would explain the dresses with big sleeves. I collect the helmet and get extra sandwiches in case it's a long time before we can get out. When I slide back under, my body goes stiff and I nearly hit my head on the table. A thin bird-like woman is sitting in our place. She's got Cruella De Vil hair and bony fingers.

The woman shoots backwards. 'What in the world?' She grabs my face and inspects it. 'Oh no.'

'Can I have my face back now please?' I ask, remembering to be polite to the stranger. 'Who are *you* hiding from?'

She drops her head. 'Maureen, you little *shit*. Why can't you just stay out of this?'

How does she know my name? Also, she owes 50p to the swear jar.

'You've ruined everything. You weren't supposed to use the button until your tenth birthday, and you can't be ten yet.' This woman is holding her own helmet, but it's the same size as mine even though her head is much bigger.

'Who…?'

'You!' she snaps. 'I'm you, you little idiot.'

What a funny name.

She frowns. 'Not this again. Just when I thought I couldn't get any more miserable.'

Mr. Smiggles clears his throat. 'This may take a while.'

I'm a little bit confused. Mr. Smiggles knows the woman and the woman knows me. But who is she?

'My name is Maureen Silverwood,' the woman says. '*You* from the future.'

I thought we were in 1999. The past is confusing.

She starts to cry. 'I can't get anything right.'

I remember to pinch myself this time, but I'm still not dreaming. What have I got us into by pressing the button?

The doors open and the guests take their seats. The old me keeps crying and then reaches down and takes all the sandwiches I brought. She pushes one into her mouth and closes her eyes.

Old Maureen is funny, but not *ha-ha* funny. At least the name Maureen suits her much better than me. When she has stopped crying, she says things like 'romantic notions' and 'perpetual patriarchy'. Isn't she happy to be at Mummy and Daddy's wedding?

Mr. Smiggles tells us the coast is clear, so I collect the helmets and we all scramble out into the gardens. I hope they don't find out we took the sandwiches. Old Maureen rests by a tree and lights a cigarette. I'd like to tell on her, but she's the only adult around.

'Things don't always turn out the way you hoped,' she says between puffs. 'Being a councilwoman in Birmingham is not the glamorous end of politics. The West Midlands is a dump.' She scratches her eczema, which is much worse than mine. 'Let's just say Prince Charming turns out to be more like Prince Arsehole.'

At least he's a prince.

She carries on at about a million miles an hour, '— And you'll discover that even well into the future, the glass ceiling in politics is real.'

I look for a glass ceiling but there's just sky. I ask Old Maureen if it's *her* first timetrip too.

She swallows and looks like she is going to cry again. 'It's about my hundredth. And I'm sick of running into you and your stupid talking cat.'

Wait. There are *other* versions of me too? When I ask what her time tripping mission is, she says I wouldn't understand. 'I *might*,' I say. 'Last week, I came second in the geography fair.'

She smiles. 'You forget, I was there. There were only three entrants because the rest of the school were watching the football team.'

Well, it's the taking part that counts. She tells me I'll get used to coming second. Her makeup is so smudged she looks like the singer in one of the rock bands Mummy likes.

'I can't believe I have to explain this *again*,' she says. 'Just my luck that I run into a Maureen on her first ever trip.'

As long as it's a quick explanation. I've got to go home for dinner soon.

She turns towards me. 'I've been trying to erase our history.'

I suddenly wish I had brought my rounders bat and Greta's Judo suit. It's dangerous here.

'I've waited a long time to press that button. Fifty goddamn years since their wedding. I won't let you and the cat ruin everything.'

That's right. Fifty is important. It's the Earth district Robotix comes from. She always travels fifty something — seconds, days or light years.

Maureen sighs. 'I was going to stop our parents before they—'

'Before I lived in Mummy's tummy?'

She brings a hand to her forehead. 'Urgh. I didn't know I was going to have to do the whole 'Birds and the Bees' thing too.'

After a difficult explanation with a diagram on a napkin, I see what she means. She's trying to stop us from being born. She's tried lots of times but every time she does, she bumps into a different version of me and Smiggles, and we save the day.

Back in the tent, the guests are queueing up for the buffet now. They're saying things like 'decent spread, eh?' and 'no chicken goujons?' As I'm trying to think how many times I need to press the buttons on the helmets to return to my own life, Old Maureen grabs her helmet and tries to take mine. She stares at me like an owl looking at its dinner. 'Let me end this,' she says.

'Hey!' I grip on tight to my G50 and it drops onto the floor. It's all muddy now.

She jams her helmet on and presses the button. Then, she's gone. That was quick.

'Mr. S,' I say, looking around. 'We need to follow Old Maureen.'

He races out from the bush he's under as I scramble to put the helmet on. There are leaves in it, and it smells foresty. Smiggles stands on top of my foot and I press the button on the helmet. The tall trees drop away and we shoot off.

***

The button doesn't take us home. Every time I press it, we visit a different Maureen. They all need help. One needs to graduate from De Montfort Technical College, one of them needs to avoid getting married to a man with a bad moustache, and one of them lives in Ireland on a farm. I want to visit more exotic places like Benidorm, but the helmet has other ideas. Maybe once we've helped fifty future versions of me, we can finally get home for dinner. I ask Mr. Smiggles if we'll be back in time to watch Animatronix? He says he hopes so, then I could understand alternate timelines better.

When the colours slow and we arrive at our next appointment with future me, we fall down onto a hard seat. The lounge we're in is tiny. I know we are high up because I can see lots of other skyscrapers. It's got a marble floor and lots of compartments to keep everything locked away. The letter on the table is addressed to 'Goodbye', so I don't open it.

We hear a noise from another room, a sort of squeak. Someone could be in trouble, but then again they could be having toilet trouble, in which case I should knock. The bathroom door is open and the noise is coming from inside. Mr. Smiggles puts his big head through the gap, then shoots up in the air like that time Greta threatened him with a cucumber.

I push the door open, but it bangs against the bath and comes back towards me. When I look through, I see something very scary, but I don't run.

243

There is a thin woman in the bath, held up by a line of fairy lights around her neck. She's naked and her skin is all flappy. It's the same Maureen from the wedding. She has the same beaky nose and white-streak in her hair. Her face is blue, apart from the red blotches of eczema. They haven't found a cure for everything in the future.

'Grrrgghh,' she says.

I freeze. A shower is a strange place to hang up decoration lights. Daddy says that electricity and water don't mix.

'Help her!' shouts Smiggles, so I jump into the bath and hold her legs.

She's heavy and she kicks her legs about. Luckily, she hasn't turned the shower on, so it's not wet. She scrambles up on my back to get a breath. Her bony ankles dig in. Old Maureen grabs the shower curtain, unhooks the fairy lights and we both come crashing down into the bath.

We lie there. The flat is completely quiet apart from our breathing. Old Maureen rubs her neck and tries to cover herself up. She takes big breaths. I get out of the bath and we look at each other. Smiggles backs into the corner and Maureen curls up into a hedgehog position. I'm sad, but not as sad as her. Best to fold up the shower curtain and put it away.

She finally speaks, but she doesn't say thank you. Her voice is all metallic like Robotix. 'Why won't you let me die?'

This is an easy question. 'You can't hurt yourself, Old Maureen. That's naughty.'

She covers herself with a white towel and squeezes past me to the medicine cabinet. Her neck has deep purple lines, and she has a small cut.

I tell her I like her flat. It's very tidy. No one says anything.

'Fairy lights, Maureen. Really? That's a new one,' says Smiggles. 'I thought the lounge wall seemed a little bare.'

Old Maureen ignores him and opens the cupboard, then she says a lot of bad words. A lot. 'Ah yes,' she croaks, 'I forgot, one of you removed my painkillers last week when I got a bit too pill-happy.' She sighs, and sits down on the toilet. 'A fat lot of good that helmet ever did me — travelling through time only to be thwarted by a primary school know-nothing and a talking furball.'

Mr. Smiggles rubs himself against her legs and Maureen starts to cry again, but she doesn't have any makeup to get smudged this time.

'I know how to make tea,' I say.

'Just go, or I'll smash that bloody helmet of yours and you'll be stuck with me forever.'

'Do you have any anti-sceptic cream for your neck?'

The corners of her eyes turn up into a smile. 'It's *antiseptic*.'

Old Maureen stands up and goes towards the kitchen. She didn't answer about the tea, but I think she meant 'yes please.'

'Do you have any tuna for Mr. S?'

Old Maureen says the world doesn't have any more tuna so he'll have to make do with fish substitute. She quickly takes the letter off the table in the lounge before we sit down with our tea.

***

I haven't pressed the red button for a long time. We've stayed with Old Future Maureen because we're helping her.

The future is funny, but not *ha-ha* funny. Everyone in Birmingham lives in high flats. There's not much room for all the people. Maureen showed me around the city, but Mr. Smiggles had to stay behind because no one has invented talking cats yet. Everything else *has* been invented though — machines for cleaning the air, machines for cleaning the machines that clean the air, and also chocolate forks. Robots do lots of jobs now, but there aren't any robot councilwomen because Maureen says they aren't stupid enough to take the job. She acts like Mummy when she's at home by cleaning and bossing me around, but she doesn't remember when a eight-and-a-half-year-old's bedtime is, so I stay up late.

Maureen takes off her scarf. Her bruises are getting better now. She lights up her electronic cigarette and inhales.

'Old Maureen?' I say.

'I told you to stop calling me that.'

'Can you show us how to get the episodes of Animatronix on the projector again? The ones I haven't seen.'

She says she needs to dial in the food order first. I've stopped asking about dinner. It's always something new, and if I don't like it, I just eat the cutlery instead. Turkey dinosaurs must have gone extinct in the future.

We watch a really good episode of Animatronix where Robotix saves the last grasshopper on the planet. Maureen complains a lot during the program but I know she likes it really.

'Why on Earth doesn't she timetrip and breed the insect again?' asks Mr. Smiggles.

'Probably because some little twerp would turn up and scupper her plans, eh?' Old Maureen pushes my shoulder.

The door system tells us the food is here. Through the video screen, I see that the delivery person is wearing a golden helmet.

Old Maureen opens the door. The girl in the helmet has a green parka like my sister's. There's a brown and white cat on the floor next to her. It's Donkey-Kong! Mr. Smiggles arches his back and hisses.

'Get a move on, Slo-Mo,' the cat says. 'We 'aven't got all night.'

The girl takes off her golden helmet. Greta!

'You are *such* a copycat,' I say, although I'm secretly pleased to see her. 'Did you bring the food?'

She turns towards Old Maureen. 'Well, you did a good job here, but I need your help back in the present.'

I don't get to decide anything. It's always Greta, or the helmet, or even Mr. Smiggles who tells me where to go. I tell her my button doesn't work.

'Urgh. Don't you know anything about time travel? You work for the good of the Universe, not the other way round.'

I think The Universe is fine here. There are dial-up dinners and chocolate forks.

Donkey-Kong prods my leg and makes a coughing sound. 'Yeah, we're 'aving some sort of insect problem. Gap in the food chain. You must have the answer or something.'

We just watched an episode of Animatronix about that!

Smiggles looks up at Old Maureen. 'It puts your life into perspective when the fate of the planet lies in the hands of an eight-year-old girl with a memory like a sieve.'

She tells him I'm nearly nine.

I think we've finished helping Old Maureen now. It's time to go. I say goodbye to her and her funny apartment. She gives me a nice hug. 'You can visit us any time with *your* G50,' I say.

She shakes her head. 'You know, Maureen, I used to be addicted to time travel, but that's all in the past now.'

I thought Mr. Smiggles said she used to be addicted to painkillers. The future is confusing.

Greta and I put on our helmets, pick up our cats and press the button one more time.

Circles

We sit cross-legged on the sand — twelve of us, not thirteen. Each member of the circle holds a drum, and we listen to the pounding of the waves. A lantern flickers in the middle. Tonight, I must lead the group and there's only one story I can tell: that of the turtle.

'Olga may be gone, but she lives on through this fable. She is the salt in the air, the sounds of the shore and the colours of the setting sun.'

Juan and Lupita look up to check if she's returned, but of course, she hasn't. The rest of the group bow their heads.

'Upon her back was a birthmark, around the size of an orange. It was an oval with leaf shapes on either side, the sign of the turtle.'

They listen as the words rise into the night air.

'Her death was not an end but the realisation of a cycle. She was swept out to the great Pacific ocean off Punta Cometa, as are the turtles we release each year. Olga had swum there every day for years. She was strong, she knew the waters and they knew her. The street dogs she fed ran up and down the beach, barking for days. That's how we knew she was gone. It was her time to transform into the myth we tell.'

The story flows just as our tears did during these last days. I pause and look at the faces of the group members. Their eyes shine through the dark. Juan and Lupita are smiling, hanging on my every word.

'She was not from Mexico,' I continue, 'but the shopkeepers, the *colectivo* drivers, the marine biologists, the fishermen and the schoolchildren came to tell us they were sorry. We told them to be glad they knew her.'

Olga was part of Mazunte. She had found an empty house with no roof and made it her own — waterproofed it, built a shower, and planted a garden.

'*Rancho Redondo* has helped many travellers passing through, including all of the lost souls that now call this place home.'

Arnaud taps his djembe drum and it calls out into the night with its low boom. Ali and Kacey join in, and suddenly the whole group is playing a cycle. The rhythms and patterns punctuate the story and connect it to this place and time. Olga used to say 'stories are domesticated, but myths are wild'. She shared this gift with us, and we still form this circle every night.

When the drum cycle finishes, I begin the next section. 'Through her relationships, she showed compassion and understanding. Olga would talk to locals about their family, their past, their homes. Conversation was her currency, and through the building of trust, she created a life for our group.'

No second house, no electricity, and no drugs — that was her deal with the police. She offered free classes, extra pairs of hands to clean up the excesses of *Semana Santa*, and made handicrafts to sell in the shops. In return, the people gave clothes, gas for the stove and building materials. Some supplied rice, beans and fruit, others gave rides in their trucks or medical supplies.

'We live in a system where no money changes hands. In this way, we co-exist with the people and landscape, and together we share these stories, these little pinpricks of eternity.'

Drums

While we play, I pray that our relationships with the local community don't fade with her memory. I lift my finger to pause the drums. 'Our sanctuary is temporary,' I say. 'This place may not be our home forever, but the circle we have built here is eternal.'

We are all running from something. Juan left his family back in Monterrey, Ali fled her six-figure college debt, and Arnaud was given six months to live. He's been here for nine. Me? I botched my exams and ran from my own failure.

'When Olga started her journey, she had no destination, nor a time limit in which to finish. She believed trips where you return home only tell you what you already know, but open journeys show you what you don't.'

She rode horses on the open plains of Patagonia, took a boat up the great Amazon river, and worked in an orphanage in Ecuador, all the time loosening the tethers that bound her to the closed-minded world she came from. News, transaction, and fear.

'In the mountains of Northern Chile, her 'other self' died. She undertook a four-day deprivation experience in which she saw the very dimension of time unlocked. She compared it to psychedelics. The hidden patterns of nature that had always been there, were suddenly accessible.'

Some nod in understanding.

'She saw her birth, her journey and her death all at once. The shaman told her that she would reach the end of her life when she had helped others on their journeys. Now that is so.'

After that, Olga had travelled north, riding the Pan-American Highway, through the cloud forests of Costa Rica, and around lake Ometepe in Nicaragua. Sometimes she went cold and hungry. Sometimes she walked for miles. She was alone.

'Depending on the season, she worked in the fields, rode out storms in the ports of the Caribbean, and cared for children whose homes were lost. Over the years, she traced the fabric of the shifting stories that ran through each place, connecting the Earth, just as the continental plates do.'

I take a moment to remember my first week at *Rancho Redondo* and find a lump building in my throat. She was so calm and open. Olga told me that four days was all it would take for the 'old me', the one who was scared and ashamed, to die. Of course, she was right. By looking at the others in the group battling tears, I could tell that they too were remembering their old selves.

When I am able to regain composure, my voice is quieter, almost a whisper. 'She arrived at Mazunte during the festival, where the town releases hundreds of baby turtles from the sanctuary back into the ocean.' It's a great celebration, but in reality, only a few of the turtles will make it to adulthood.

'That year, hundreds of spectators watched on the beach. A Mexican news channel interviewed Olga and she showed the camera her birthmark. The sanctuary gave her the honour of releasing the first turtle into the water.'

I feel Ali's hand slip into mine. The rest of the group smile at the thought of our beloved turtles.

'If her parents were watching, they would not have recognised their daughter. Her hair was brilliant white, bleached by the sun. Her skin was an earthy red and her green eyes turned to grey.

'Summer changed to autumn and the crowds drifted away. *La Dama Tortuga* stayed.'

One by one, we arrived and built our group around her. Without Olga, it is doubtful that the police will hold up their end of the bargain. Municipal politicians might seek to win votes by evicting the 'hippies' from *Rancho Redondo.* If we do not leave soon, immigration might be called, or the police. Or worse.

I take a handful of sand and let it drain through my fingers. The breeze whips the grains out over the water. 'But like us, she was running. Running from loss.'

The story, which was flowing so smoothly, now falters. Everyone in the group knows of her personal tragedy. It makes them respect her even more. As with any loss, saying the words out loud heals. Our circle heals.

'At nineteen, she had travelled across the Atlantic to study in Santiago, Chile, and it was on a university trip to the mountains of Torres del Paine that she met her soulmate. When she saw the clear reflection of the rocky peaks in the lakes, she knew she had discovered the other half of her.'

Illapa came from a village in the mountains of Northern Chile near the border with Peru. He was naive in the ways of big cities, and his classmates referred to him as The Alpaca because of his curly hair.

'Illapa possessed a rich understanding of the Earth. When they watched the stars, he told Olga that where *her* people mapped dots of light, the Aymara saw the shapes of deep black between them — the mother, the llama, the snake. Their group sat around the campfire they built each night, and he recounted the myths of these animals and of the people that lived among them. The words travelled out into the forests and glaciers. While all of the students listened, only Olga understood. By the time they returned to Santiago, they felt like they had lived an entire life together and Olga was pregnant with their child.'

A truck engine starts and I pause. At this hour, it could be the police, looking for tourists to bother. The lights move off and the sound passes.

'After the birth of their child,' I say, a little quieter, 'Olga returned to finish her studies. Illapa

256

travelled back to his village with the baby, and Olga would follow when her course ended. The Alpaca and his son travelled by boat, following the Chilean coastline from Valparaiso up past the port of Antofagasta. During the night, a freak wave capsized the boat and it sank to the bottom of the Pacific Ocean. All fifteen souls aboard were lost.'

The poor mother didn't learn their fate until she reached the hilltop village, a week later.

'The villagers held a funeral and helped Olga through the pain of those dark days. They told her tales of Illapa and of their ancestors. Olga found strength in those stories. They were far truer than any police investigation or telephone calls from across the ocean. She learned the true meaning of his name — bringer of new weather.'

This is the perfect moment for an interlude of drums, but when I look around the circle, the faces are enraptured, caught in the power of the tale, as if Olga herself were telling it. I push on.

'The Aymara people talk of the past as in front of them, and the future as behind. In her months there, Olga grew from her experience, rather than shrinking from the truth of her situation. Her family bade her return to Germany, but she felt that turning back would not help her to complete the journey she started.'

According to the village shaman, Olga needed guidance on how to continue. He suggested she go on the four-day quest to reconnect with the Earth.

'So, Olga sat atop a mountain with no food or water for four days. She took nothing but a blanket. On the fourth day, she died. That's how *she* put it. When she saw the sunrise after three nights alone, the part of her that could exist in the Western World had died. Her possessions, fears and dreams were only three days deep.'

We had all experienced something similar here. Medical college was my parents dream, not mine. They would never understand my life here. But, after four days participating in the circle, I had found the peace that eternal truth brings. I told my family I couldn't go back. Perhaps Olga's death and the difficulties that will follow shall mark the start of another journey for me.

'Olga came from the sea. She was born in a commune on an island in the Indian Ocean, to German parents. Yet, before her memories of that place made their mark, the authorities shut it down over a fishing dispute. They broke up a community that had existed in peace for years. The 'foreigners' were deported back to their countries of birth, and the fishing companies fought over the remains like snapping sharks.'

As her biological parents had no money and no fixed address, she was taken from them and raised by a 'proper family'.

The temperature has dropped and I feel a chill on my arms. I wonder how many of the group were forced out of *their* families.

'Olga's new family lived inland, in a cold city with tall buildings. Though they cared for Olga, her parents pushed her down the path to success as if it were a straight line — a sensible education, a serious career and a house to put all of her things in. As she grew into an adult, Olga began to notice the little pinpricks of reality that peaked in from the edges of her vision. They were always harder to see in the city, but she seemed to find peace and truth whenever she felt the sea air or looked at the views from the top of a mountain.'

Lupita drapes a scarf over my shoulders. It's been a few minutes since we warmed our hands on the drums and a few members of the group are feeling the chill of the night. I go on.

'After years of protecting her from the truth, her parents agreed to remove her blinkers. They told Olga that she was German, but that she did not come from there. She was not shocked. Olga had always felt like she needed to know other places in the world to understand who she was. She went to Santiago to study and never looked back, for like the Aymara, she saw the great truths of her past as existing in front of her, not behind.'

Arnaud is crying. Juan is locked in a tight embrace with Lupita. Others look to the sky. Her death is still raw, but we maintain her legacy in this place by building these memories. I stand and pick up some driftwood. Walking around the outside of the group, I draw a line.

We say the next part together, as we do each night. 'This line does not enclose us, but we live together within it, wherever it may be. It represents our journey and our stories. It represents our connection with each other and with the myths of the earth on which we stand.'

Our circle is infinitely small and unimaginably large. It exists in all places. I utter the last line of Olga's story. 'By drawing the tale of the turtle girl to an end, we complete her circle.'

The waves pound the shore, the wind blows over the palm roofs and the drums begin again.

Home Invasion

In the winter of '95, junk invaded our neighborhood. It moved into our front yards at night and stayed. A gleaming sink appeared on my lawn with *'free to a good home'* scrawled on the wooden backing. My good home already had two sinks. Didn't everyone already have sinks?

We lived in a dead-end street where neighborhood opinions caused silent arguments. Jungle-like gardens got hacked back for parking. Community spirit moved out. "I'm not going to take it in," I said, like it was some lame puppy. The sink suffered the winter frost, losing its sheen to dirt and grit. When it rained, birds dive bombed from the sycamore trees to wash.

Next spring, an exhausted printer dumped itself, cables sprawled, toner bleeding out on the grass. Printers were luxury items back then. This was before the junk learned about Craigslist. I cleaned the leaves from the slot and left a fifty dollar Monopoly bill with a note: *Federal Mint of Freedom Drive.* In less than a week, the note was gone, but the printer festered.

Soon, other household items came to live on our grass, creeping in the dark, still in the light. Electro-shocked toasters, fractured picture frames, misfiring super-soakers, broken-down carts — all free to a good home. For a while, we fought it, then we bargained with it, tried to love it. It didn't love us back.

An entire white picket fence rained down on my neighbours garden. I suggested donating it. Instead they replaced their fence with the new panels and left the dirty ones in their place. Six weeks was all it took for poison ivy to creep its way over their prize fence.

Next, a truck propped itself on bricks outside number 25. Where would they park now? Incredibly, it had a key and the engine turned over. A tank full of gas and nowhere to go. The guy was furious, marching around, demanding a neighborhood sting operation to catch the phantom dumper. Like it was all one guy. The scrapyard charged to remove trucks, so the guy waited for wheels to turn up in front of someone else's garage.

And still it continued. Every night, new recruits joined the ranks of redneck treasure. Green verges and tall sycamores battled with jagged shrapnel and rust. When it rained, old sofas soaked it up like sponges. They rotted.

We ran yard sales and negotiated with the city. No use. The residents no longer had sidewalks and gardens, but junkyards bolted onto their homes. Amputee trailers, wounded power tools, withered goodwill parcels, and cracked glass; all the town's burdens offloaded onto us.

Eventually, City Hall claimed the land and rehoused us on a dead-zone lot where nothing survived. The flowers we nurtured now creep through the debris of Freedom Drive in search of light.

Sometimes, we drive back to look at war between nature and the bones of society. We search for survivors. You can find anything there. *Free to a good home.*

Acknowledgements

Publications in which the stories first featured are listed below:

The Idea of Eve, Write Festival Anthology
Don Pedro's Dog, The Cabinet of Heed Issue 21
Peloton, Flash Fiction Magazine
Falling Down, East of The Web
The Church of Rainbow, Fabula Argentea
Townies, New Pop Lit
The Anatomy of a Hurdy-Gurdy, FlashBack Fiction
Home Invasion, Bending Genres 23
Racing Fate, The Lit Quarterly Issue 4
Time and Time Again, Sci-Fi Lampoon Issue 2
Ludgate Circus Crossing, MTP Summer Anthology 2020
Beautiful Destruction, Ellipsis Zine
The Fisherwoman, Loft Books Anthology
Hello, You, Literary Yard
The Quiet Cosmonaut, Sundial Magazine
The Matchstick House, East of The Web
Saudade, Janus Literary Wild Dark Sea Anthology
Cherry Orchards, appeared as *A Simulation* in All World's Wayfarer X

Windows Explorer Cannot Process This Request, Janus Literary

Marbles and Memories, MTP 2020 Competition Anthology

Satellite of Love, NFFD Flash Flood

Triple Word Score, Fiction on The Web

A Silent Songbird, The Literatus Issue III

Two Minutes, *Forty-Six Seconds*, appeared as *It's Not My Place* in Gabba Gabba Hey a Ramones Anthology, Fahrenheit Press

Consuming Life, Idle Ink

Circles, The Winnow

Happysad, Storgy

Two Nights Only, Vigorous Roots Anthology, Ooligan Press

Thanks

I am truly grateful to everyone who has contributed to the publication of the book. This includes anyone who has read, listened to, or provided feedback on these stories. This includes the editors of all the previously listed publications who have selected my work to offer their readers and the wider writing community, who are always so supportive.

Special mentions go to the following people:

Gaynor Jones and Neil Clarke (both fantastic authors in their own right) for reading the book and providing such kind and supportive quotes.

Rikki Dunmore for creating the beautiful artwork for the cover. You can see more of his work on his blog: rikkidunmore.tumblr.com/

Will Bidder for his support in proofreading the manuscript.

The Alpha Writers group for inspiring me to show up at the writing desk.

About

Philip Charter is a British writer who teaches writing to non-native English speakers. He is the author of two short fiction collections, *Foreign Voices* and *The Fisherwoman and other stories*. His work has been featured in numerous publications and has won or placed in competitions such as the Loft Books Short Story Competition, The Janus Literary Anthology Prize, and the Oxford Flash Fiction prize.

Also by Philip Charter: *Foreign Voices*

An amateur cyclist crashes in the middle of the Atlas Mountains, an immigrant house sitter fights to save his boss from dangerous thugs, and a satanist florist sets up shop in a sleepy English town. These stories all contain characters who are out of place, or at least out of their comfort zone. In this collection, Philip Charter explores a variety of themes through the eyes of engaging characters with foreign voices.

Foreign Voices is available via philipcharter.com and Amazon.

Printed in Great Britain
by Amazon